Diamond Girl

Joni Harrison

Published by Joni Harrison, 2019.

DIAMOND GIRL

First edition. September 12, 2019.

Written by Joni Harrison.

Also by Joni Harrison

The Peacekeeper
The World Between Worlds

Standalone
Diamond Girl

Watch for more at https://www.joniharrison.com.

To Granny, who started me on this path. And Mickey, who saw me through.

Chapter 1

June 1973

The heat stifled in the Lakeview Club's dance studio. The sun flared off the floor-to-ceiling mirrors and drenched the short waltz class in hot light. I edged closer to the window, hoping to catch a waft of the faint breeze and tugged at my sweaty leotard, stretching the sticky material away from my prickling skin. I wanted to tear the stupid thing off and run away screaming. But dance classes were mandatory for debutantes and that's what Mama and Daddy had decided I would be.

At least today I was cutting out early. Ten more minutes until we made our escape. I searched out my best friend Peggy Harmon across the room. She was easy to spot, her riot of honey curls gleaming in the sunlight. I pointed out the time and she winked one of her saucer-sized baby blues at me, nudging Nancy Bell beside her. Nancy pretended to be absolutely riveted by ancient Mrs. Popple's short waltz instructions.

The Popps droned on, impervious to the heat in her dated navy rayon skirted suit, her granite hair twisted and pinned tightly to her head. The rumor was that she'd been a Ziegfeld Follies dancer in her heyday, but you'd be hard-pressed to find an ounce of joy in the deep frown lines around her mouth and her militant adherence to the rules of etiquette.

Peggy elbowed Nancy again but she ignored us, smoothing down her precious long curtain of dark, Ali McGraw hair. That kiss-ass could stay here if she wanted. It was no skin off my nose if Nancy didn't come — even if she did play a decent left field.

Our debut at the annual Cotillion Ball was in less than two months. Everyone who cared about that kind of nonsense said this year's dance was going to be *the* event of the social calendar. The Cotillion Society had blown the decor budget out of the park because Mama insisted they absolutely needed to have lilies instead of the regular cheap-looking carnations. When the planning committee wavered, Mama gave them her best first-runner-up in the 1950 Miss South Carolina pageant smile and offered to pay the difference.

"A young woman's debut is one of the most special events of her life," Mama said in her musical voice. "We want to make it a night our girls never forget."

The blue hairs had no choice but to give in. As the only genuine Southern Belle in the ranks of teeny tiny Elmhurst, Ohio's Cotillion Society, Mama had established herself as the authority on how things were done. Also, the committee felt bad for her. Everyone knew that Kathleen had run off before Mama could see her make her debut.

Eight more minutes until we caught the bus. I visualized my turn at bat, saw myself connecting with the sweet spot and skying the ball over the heads of those Cleveland city snobs to win the state championship. And maybe if some college scouts were in the crowd and liked what they saw, I could even keep playing after this year. I shook my head. That fantasy was too unrealistic to even entertain.

"Isn't that right, Miss Bennet?" Mrs. Popple asked, interrupting my daydream.

"Um, yes?" I replied.

Shoot. One more wrong answer I was going to end up in debutante detention and then our plan was never going to work.

"As I was saying, make sure to keep your head up and a smile on your face," The Popps said, demonstrating a grin that showed off her dentures to full effect. "Thanks to Mr. Bennet's connections, we have secured quite a notable photographer for the ball. He will be taking your photo while you are dancing, so you want to make sure that you are always prepared to have your picture taken. That means no looking down at your feet. I am talking especially to you, Bobby Rice."

Bobby shifted uncomfortably and the tips of his jug ears turned pink. He pushed his oversized thick-framed glasses up the bridge of his nose and bowed his head. There were scattered giggles. Boys didn't go to Deb class, but Bobby's mother enrolled him anyway. She made it perfectly clear that not only would he learn to dance, but he would also serve as someone's escort for the ball. And what Cecilia Rice wanted, she got. Too bad Bobby was a lost cause. As if holding his clammy hands weren't bad enough, there was always a good chance you'd get a kick to the shin or a crushed toe from his constant missteps.

"Make sure to thank your father for me, Miss Bennet. We are so grateful to his friends," Mrs. Popple said.

Was she ever going to stop talking?

"I will," I replied. Daddy's "friends" were actually just people who did him favors because he owned a large steel company in the city where lots of people from town worked.

Three more minutes to launch.

The Popps paired us off to work through our steps. Instantly, a bubble of space formed around Bobby as girls avoided his pleading eyes. No one wanted the lemon partner. Bobby blushed even harder than he had when Mrs. Popple called him out.

Aw, hell. Even if Bobby was a rotten dancer, we were all stuck in this nightmare together. I gritted my teeth and strode over to him.

"Bobby, would you do me the honor of this dance?" I asked in my most polite, well-brought-up deb voice.

He nodded and took my hand. The Popps started the record and my toes were practically mush within the first minute of the song.

"I-I'm sorry, Bliss," Bobby stammered as his grip turned even more slippery. "You look pretty today, as usual."

"Thank you, Bobby," I said.

He was a sweet boy and a brain to boot. If he could just get his act together, he was sure to be a catch in a few years.

Peggy and her partner brushed past us and she managed to land a gentle elbow in my side. That was my cue. Peggy and Nancy were waiting for my lead but I didn't want Bobby to think I was running from him. Surely the song had to end soon?

I kept dancing while Nancy tried to get my attention. Her elbow was less gentle.

"Let's go!" She hissed.

I stubbornly waltzed on. I didn't care if we were late. I was at least going to let Bobby have one damn shame-free dance, broken toes or not.

It was ridiculous that we'd be banned from the ball if we missed these dumb deb training classes. The Elmhurst Lady Scarlets' first State Championship appearance counted as a high priority in my books, but The Popps (and Mama and Daddy) thought softball was nothing more than a kids' game. Not men's baseball though, go figure.

Finally, finally, finally, the music ended. I immediately hunched over, faking extreme pain.

"Ohhhh, ohhhh," I groaned.

"My God, Bliss. Are you okay?" Bobby asked, hovering over me.

"Thank you for the dance, but I need Peggy," I said, waving him off. "Peggy!"

Peggy rushed over. "I'm here Bliss."

Mrs. Popple hobbled over, hands on hips.

"What is happening here?" She asked.

"My Aunt Flo is in town," I said. "It just hurts so bad."

The Popps hushed me. "Say no more, Miss Bennet. We are in mixed company. You may be excused for the afternoon. Miss Harmon can escort you home."

"Wait, I am their ride! I have to drive them," Nancy said, her rehearsed lines stiff. I'm not sure it would be possible for her to act as if she cared less. I rolled my eyes at Peggy while Mrs. Popple's back was turned. Her dimples deepened with suppressed laughter. The whole scheme was Peggy's idea, but no one suspects the girl with the round, angelic face and rosy cheeks to be the mastermind.

"Well now, I'm not sure we need two girls to help Miss Bennet," The Popps said, hesitating.

Oh no, we were going to blow this. I doubled over again.

"Ohhhh, it hurts so bad! Why are women cursed? I wish I never got my stupid pe-"

The Popps's face purpled in horror. She truly believed the floor would open up and swallow us whole if I said the word period in the presence of the opposite sex.

"Girls, please help Miss Bennet home. Immediately."

Peggy and Nancy helped pick me up off the parquet floor and supported my weight as I limped out of the studio. On the way, I caught Bobby's eye and winked. Good luck, he mouthed back. Bobby was no fool.

As soon as we were out of eyesight, Nancy threw my arm off her shoulders. Nancy's tiny rosebud mouth and pert little nose always reminded me of a bunny's cute face. Though anyone who'd ever had one of those suckers as a pet knew that they could be mean. Nancy was the same. Adorable features, sharp bite.

"Could you have taken any longer?" She asked. "We're going to be late."

Nancy's brand-new candy apple colored Firebird sat shining in the club's parking lot. Peggy whistled low. The car was a graduation present from her parents, Nancy smugly told us.

"Nice, isn't it?" She said.

Nancy Bell never missed a chance to show off. She'd been doing it since we were kids. If Nancy weren't on the team, I'd gladly have nothing to do with her. But because she was, I tried to get along.

We sped off to Elmhurst High and Nancy screeched to a halt in the parking lot. My public school was a source of constant scandal for Mama, but in a town as small as Elmhurst, there weren't a lot of options. St. Bernadette's was the only private school in town, and Daddy said he'd be damned if he got his daughter mixed in with those Catholics just for the sake of a uniform.

We ran to the team bus in our dance leotards, gear bags in hand. Our assistant coach, Jem Robinson, waited by the door in the hot sun, sweat beading on his forehead and clipboard in hand. His tall, muscular body was rigid with impatience. He ticked our names off with extra venom.

"You're late," he said. "And it is too damn hot to be standing out here."

"I thought you people were made for the heat," Nancy said running her finger down his bare, ebony-colored arm.

Jem glowered and shook her off. Nancy giggled and sashayed past him.

"Ignorant," Jem muttered.

Embarrassed, I didn't reply or make eye contact. Jem was the only black person I'd ever met. All I knew was that Daddy didn't think it was right that he was hanging around us girls on the team. I supposed Jem was fine, except for his constant foul mood. Why did Nancy have to get him going right before the game?

I climbed the bus stairs and refocused. The avocado green leather seats smelled like stale gym socks with a hint of Charlie perfume. Normally I held my breath until I adjusted to the stench of the old clunker, but not this time. If it was going to be my last ride, I wanted to take it all in.

"Everyone is finally here," Jem told Coach Christie.

Coach was hunched over the wheel, double-checking the map. He was still pretty fit for a man Daddy's age, with only the tiniest bit of beer belly that stretched out his ringer tee with our school name. I liked Coach. He was a plain talker with dark hair graying at the temples and kind eyes that crinkled in the corners when you did something to make him happy. Like, smack the ball hard.

Satisfied with our route, Coach closed the door and honked twice.

"All aboard for the State Championship Express!"

My stomach lurched and tightened. This time the pang in my guts wasn't imaginary. It was time to focus on winning.

Chapter 2

"Any news yet, Bliss?" Coach hollered back at me while we were on the road. He was as anxious as I was to hear something.

"Nope. And there's no point dwelling on it," I said.

Because I'd never be able to go anyway.

To ease my nerves, I gave the team a once-over. Hairspray was thick in the air as we primped. It was a pre-game tradition to perfect hair and makeup. Extra special sparkly crimson and white game day ribbons curled and adorned matching high ponytails.

Even the twins Susie and Deb had managed to tame their normally chaotic waves. Cher must have ironed their hair ahead of time. Her mother ran the beauty salon and she took care of all team styling. She couldn't open a can of coke with her extra-long peach nails, but somehow she managed to do hair, makeup and hold down second base.

"Looking sharp, ladies," I said to the twins.

"Thank you," they replied in unison. "Cher did it."

I smiled and tried to guess which one was Susie and which one was Deb. Four years on the same team and the only time I knew for certain who was who was when they were standing in position on the field. Susie played third base and Deb was first. Their inseparable twin bond made for a formidable infield defence but their tendency to speak as one made for creepy conversations that I usually tried to avoid off the field.

"Heads up!" Cher called out.

She tossed me, Peggy, and Nancy our new ribbons with a wink while she made her way over to Sharon's seat. Sharon had recently made the ill-informed decision to copy Jane Fonda's shag with her own kitchen shears. Backup pitcher Tessa had her birdlike arm slung across Sharon's shoulders, telling her it wasn't that bad. Cher's purple eyeshadow creased in concern while she examined Sharon's uneven bangs.

Thank the Good Lord for ribbons. The only reason Mama had let me play softball for this long was that she thought they were just darling and approved of the extra makeup we wore on game day. Any sport that encouraged a triple layer of mascara was just fine in her books, up to a point.

Just to make sure that I was always maintaining my ladylike dignity, Mama had put together a special travelling makeup kit for my gear bag. I left it at home to make room for my latest read, a history of the Indians' World Series wins. I used a picture of me and Michael from winter formal as the bookmark. I liked to take it out and marvel at my handsome boyfriend in his midnight velvet tuxedo, his high cheekbones and easy grin projecting confidence. It was still so hard to believe that he had chosen me.

I smiled. It was time to get fired up. I did a lap of the bus, high-fiving everyone up and down the aisle while Coach yelled at me to sit down. Everyone got a palm-stinging slap.

Everyone except Becca Porter. I left her hand dangling in the hair like a dead fish and shook my head.

"No way," I said.

Becca pouted and fluttered her extra-long fake eyelashes. Her hair was so fair it was practically white, making her real lashes just about invisible. She had a dusting of freckles over her nose and layer of baby fat that clung stubbornly to her body and face, swelling her features. Becca complained that if she didn't draw her eyes in with liner and lashes she'd be stuck with nothing but two little blue beads on her face.

"Aw, come on Bliss, are you going to hold this against me forever? Coach isn't even mad about it," she said in a whiny voice.

I stiffened. "You mean, am I still pissed that our slap hit specialist intentionally missed the second-most important game of our entire high-school careers? Yeah, actually, I am."

Becca's voice took a pleading edge. "But I knew you guys would be fine without me. You won, didn't you? Besides, my Mom bought those tickets forever ago. I didn't know we'd make it that far."

"You should have."

I crossed my arms. I liked Becca, but I hated when people acted against the best interests of the team. We all had our roles to play, and driving off to the city to see dumb mop-haired David Cassidy sing to a bunch of snivelling girls was beyond selfish. You didn't always get to do what you wanted to do in life. Sometimes you had to do what was expected from you.

"I know," Becca said. "I'm sorry! I couldn't even hear anything over all that screaming anyway. I wish I had been with you guys."

I softened. "We definitely could have used you in the eighth. It was getting pretty dicey."

"I'm here now, right?" She said, a tiny note of hope in her voice.

"Because it's convenient for you," I said with a little smile.

Becca smiled back. She knew she had me.

"Bliss! What can I do to prove I'm 100% committed to this team. I'll do anything!"

"Anything?" I asked, mischievously.

Becca furrowed her brow with worry.

Ten minutes later, she stood in the front of the bus in her sports bra and pants, her upper body completely graffitied with team slogans. RED HOT was scrawled across her midsection in bright red felt marker. That was my special touch.

"Cheer! Cheer! Cheer!" We screamed.

The back of Coach's neck turned pink as he kept his eyes resolutely on the road. He'd told us many times that he "didn't like seeing any young ladies in their skivvies" but sometimes we just had to ignore him.

Jem scowled in the front seat, his broad shoulders hunched over. He winced as our shrieks grew louder. His wide, open face wasn't made for frowning, but that's all he seemed to do around us. I wasn't sorry for him for a second. If he didn't want to get stuck coaching the girls' softball team, he shouldn't have flunked out of gym class. It was ludicrous, the school's star base-ball player, headed to UCal in the fall on a scholarship, failing Mr. Fredrick's easy-as-pie gym class of all things. I'd seen him on the field. He could have run circles around that place with a broken leg. But they'd had no choice but to flunk him when he stopped showing up. What an idiot.

Jem should have been grateful to Coach for letting him make up the extra credit by assisting instead of sulking all over the place. It made me so mad. Even if Jem had some decent hitting pointers, I hated that my team was the last resort. Just to spite him, I yelled even louder.

"Our team is what?" Becca started.

"Red hot!" We replied.

"OUR TEAM IS WHAT?"

"RED HOT!"

We all screamed the rest together:

"OUR TEAM IS R-E-D H-O-T THAT'S THE WAY YOU SPELL RED HOT, RED HOT, UH HUH, RED HOT!"

Tortured, Jem stuffed his fingers in his ears. Coach chuckled as he pulled into the gas sta-tion.

"Just going to pop in for some gas and earplugs. You need a pair, Robinson?"

"I'll take a cyanide pill if they have any," he muttered.

"Coming right up!" Coach replied. "Bennet, can you come to help me pick out the best sui-cide-aid for Robinson?"

"I thought you'd never ask." I followed Coach off the bus. "Maybe if they're out of cyanide, he could just swallow some anti-freeze?"

I turned to see if my joke had landed, but Coach's smile was gone. He'd pulled a folded sheet of paper out of his pocket.

"Do you know what this is?" He asked.

My heart sunk and my face reddened.

"I can explain," I said, with growing dread.

Why did my stupid 18th birthday have to be in October?

"Explain to me why the parent signature line of this permission slip is blank," Coach said. "The thing is, a permission slip without any permission on it is useless to me. And now I'm not going to be able to let you play."

"What?" I said. My knees buckled and I put out a hand to steady myself. "You can't bench me. Who's going to play shortstop?"

Coach shrugged. "We'll figure it out."

How could he be acting so cool when the whole game was on the line? There was no way I was going to ride the bench. "There has to be some way," I pleaded.

"Well, I suppose if you called one of your parents right now and got oral permission, I could accept that in lieu of a signature," Coach said.

My stomach knotted but I nodded like it was no big deal.

"Sure, no problem," I lied.

We walked over to the payphone and I debated which parent would be better to call.

Daddy didn't know my deb class schedule, so he wouldn't be mad about me skipping out. But the idea of him talking to Coach filled me with dread. Daddy didn't respect women's sports, and he especially didn't respect men who wasted time on them. Or at least that's the reason he gave for disliking Coach when I'd asked him.

Mama did know my schedule and she was sure to give me hell for playing hooky. The Popps would have given her the heads up that I was on my way home. She was probably sitting on her chaise lounge, stewing about how I was acting just like my sister. It was about this time of year that Kathleen had started missing a lot of deb classes too. It was so unfair. I wasn't anything like her.

Coach tapped his watch.

"Today, junior," he said.

Then again, since I was safely enrolled to attend Bryn Mawr College in September, Daddy thought his work was done.

I grabbed the phone and dialled Daddy's office.

"Sorry, sweetheart, he's off on a site tour," his secretary said in her nasal whine.

Dammit. I had to talk to Mama after all. She'd fought with Daddy last night, and I prayed she had taken one of her nerve pills this morning. I gripped the phone extra tight while I turned the numbers for home.

"Hello?" Mama answered, an edge to her voice.

"Mama, it's me," I said.

"Bliss! Sugar, where are you? Are you well? Mrs. Popple called to say you had taken ill."

I exhaled. She sounded worried, but not loopy. My stomach unclenched slightly.

"Um, I'm on my way to the city," I replied.

"You WHAT? Are you on drugs?"

"No, Mama! God! I'm with the team."

Mama and Daddy were so terrified I was going to end up like Kathleen that a tiny smidge of misbehavior put them on high alert.

"Do not take the Lord's name in vain with me, young lady. I don't care who you're out with, you just get your behind home right now."

I braced myself for what I had to ask next. "I can't Mama, we're on our way to the State finals. And the thing is, I need your permission to play in the game. Coach said you could just tell him over the phone."

I held my breath, waiting for her answer.

"Sounds like you're in quite the pickle," Mama said. "Saying no would teach you a real lesson about lying. I thought you were done with that silly game. It's time to get serious about being a proper young lady. I'm not sure Michael wants a tomboy for a girlfriend."

Mama wasn't loopy, but she did sounds spiteful. Sometimes that was worse than when she was sad.

"Please, Mama," I begged. "Don't punish the whole team because of me. Besides, how embarrassing would it be if I weren't able to play? People would start to ask questions about what was wrong with me."

There was silence on her end. I'd hit her in a tender spot: our reputation. If there was one thing Mama hated, it was to be thought of badly.

"Fine, little bird. I'll say yes, but this is the last time, you hear?"

Relief washed over me and my clenched body relaxed. But Mama wasn't done.

"In exchange, I'm signing you up for that extra etiquette class. I think you could use a refresher and we need to straighten some of that wildness out of you," she said.

I groaned. "Another etiquette class? Mama, why? You know my manners are perfect."

"If they were, you wouldn't be embarrassing me with this phone call right now. And you'll apologize to Mrs. Popple when you get home too. Now put Wilfred on the phone."

"Who's Wilfred?" I asked, clueless.

"Coach Christie, you silly goose."

Huh? I didn't even know Coach had a first name.

"Bye Mama, I love you."

"I love you too."

I passed off the phone to Coach and trudged back to the bus.

The relief of Mama's permission was short-lived. Now all I could think about was the noose of expectations tightening around my neck. The wheels were turning on Mama's perfect daughter plan and there was no room for softball in it.

Chapter 3

The heat reached its apex as we pulled up outside of Rosemount Park's diamond. My stomach knotted and unknotted as I ransacked my bag for my lucky lipstick. "Gone With the Wind" was a fierce red. I wore it in honor of the Lady Scarlets, even if Mama said that it clashed with my auburn hair.

The girls filed off the bus, nerves tight on their faces. Peggy waited for me as I panicked.

"I can't find my lipstick," I said when she beckoned me to hurry up.

"You can borrow mine, I bought the identical shade," she said.

"You know it's not the same," I replied.

I needed to find mine. I had worn it for the last six games in a row and had hit big every time. My fingers ran along the seams and rooted through the debris that hadn't been cleared from the bottom of my sack in years.

"Coach is coming back," Peggy said. "You better hurry."

I started to sweat as Coach heaved his way back up with steps.

"Bennet! Get a move on or you're riding the bench."

"I'm coming! I'm coming!" I said, but I didn't move. I couldn't go anywhere without my lucky lipstick.

Deep in the recess of an unused pocket, I came up with a tube of color. I must have put it there for safekeeping and forgotten it.

Triumphant, I applied the lipstick and stepped into the sun-crisped grass of the ball diamond. The concessions stand was doing brisk business, but today the smell of grilled hot dogs and fresh popcorn only turned my stomach.

Steps ahead of me, Peggy had launched herself in the arms of George, her waiting fiancé. His freckled face was hot in the sun and the mesh ballcap he wore over his shaggy ginger hair did nothing to protect the back of his neck from the burn that was starting to set in.

"What are you doing here?" Peggy asked.

He grinned. "I brought a little cheering section. You didn't think I was going to let my girl win the state championship without being there to watch, did you?"

Peggy kissed him shamelessly. Mama said that 18 was too young to get married, but Peggy and George were hopelessly in love. Anyway, Mama would be thrilled if I married Michael tomorrow.

"Break it up, lovebirds," Coach said. "Girls, you need to get into that dugout right now. No more fooling around. It's game time."

"Did Michael come?" I asked George, searching for his angular face in the stands.

He shook his head, apologetic.

"Sorry, Bliss. He had to work. He says he's going to pick you up from the school when the bus gets back."

I could tell Peggy was watching me for disappointment, but I was slightly relieved. Michael made it hard for me to think straight. I needed all my focus for the game tonight.

We jogged it in and followed Jem through a series of stretches. I tried not to let the Spartans' spectator section get under my skin. There were at least a hundred people decked out in kelly green holding signs. They booed when our team was introduced.

I tried to take comfort in the familiar faces in the stands. My parents weren't there, but nearly everyone else had someone to cheer for them. Becca's mother had even made a sign with David Cassidy's face and a little speech-bubble that said, "Rock me, Becca!" I caught Becca's eye and she grinned sheepishly. She really did love that silly singer.

"Listen up," Coach said as we readied to take the field. "I'm not going to get into a whole speech thing here because, frankly, you ladies don't need it. We've been working for this all season, and now the day is here. This is your game for the taking. So play smart, stay cool, and use your heads out there, goddammit! I expect a dubya today. Who's with me?"

"We are!" We shouted back.

"You have anything to add Robinson?" He asked Jem.

"Nope," Jem replied and spat out of the dugout.

"Inspiring as usual," Coach said. "Now let's get out there and bring home the Title!"

I took my place at short, bringing the practice ball with me. Before throwing it around the horn, I traced my number three times in the dirt with my right toe. The field was mine now.

One by one, I fired the ball to each infield player who tossed it back in return. Linda on the mound, her dark eyes smouldering with game-time intensity. Karen at catcher, yelling out encouragement in her authoritative, deep bark. Cher at second, her gossipy salon persona replaced with cool competence. Twins Deb and Susie mirror images of each other at first and third.

Thwap, thwap, thwap. Each time the ball came back to my glove hard and sure. My nerves melted away. This was where I belonged.

I'd been playing shortstop since I was nine years old and my little league coach told me I had Velcro in my glove and a missile for an arm. I could catch anything that came at me. Fast, short, hard, high, wild — I snagged that ball and zipped it to first with laser accuracy. I'd taken more balls to the body than I cared to remember, but I'd do anything to keep the play in front of me. Diving, leaping, sprinting, whatever it took to stop the ball. Not many people would think getting thrown from a horse would be good luck, but that's exactly how I see the day that nasty pony threw me over and squashed Mama's dreams for my dressage career. Daddy put his foot down. He wasn't going to let some dumb beast break his precious daughter's neck. At a loss for what to do with me all summer, they put me in ball. The rest is history.

Three more throws until we could get going. Jane was in right field again for Becca, her glasses glinting in the sun. Coach wasn't mad, but he did remember commitment. Peggy in center. Nancy in left. She hurled it back at me with all her strength, her long ponytail whipping with the effort.

"Nice throw," I called, pretending I couldn't feel the sting in my palm.

I tossed the ball back into our dugout and waited. The crowd jeered as Linda warmed up her arm. She was a presence on the mound, all hard lines and coppery skin, the muscles in her shoulders bulging against her jersey.

"Is that all you've got? My little sister throws harder than you and she's in primary school!" One jackass yelled.

Fool. Linda Ruiz had the fastest arm in the country. She was scouted by the Sooners in ninth grade and was headed to the University of Oklahoma on a full scholarship in the fall. And there was nothing she liked more than being underestimated.

"Hey, wetback! Go home!" Someone shouted from the stands.

That nastiness wasn't new to Linda, but she frowned like the catcalls were getting to her. She even sent the next pitch wild. The girls in Cleveland's dugout nudged each other while they watched. A few were actually grinning like they thought the pressure was getting to her. Idiots. They were getting keyed up, and jittery players were sloppy players.

The first girl stepped up to bat and whiffed the first pitch. Linda got down to work and fanned the first three. I jogged off with a smile, letting the flow of the game take over. I loved when the pitcher did all of the work for us. That should shut up those fans in green a little bit.

Sadly, the Spartans were not willing to just roll over and take a whupping. Our turn at bat came up empty, with two runners left stranded on base. I was at second when Susie popped out.

"Early days, ladies," Coach said before we took the field again. "We're wearing 'em down, getting on base. This is just the beginning. Hang in there."

I grabbed my glove and a handful of Double Bubble. I only started chewing gum after my first at-bat.

I jawed while Linda went to work on the first batter. Her pitch really was a thing of beauty, the way it combined elegance and athleticism, her perfect windmill releasing rocket after rocket. The batter chased strike two low and outside. The trick was to get in a few solid pitches so they were expecting something they could hit and then start tossing junk. Sure, we'd get behind the count if the batter didn't take the bait, but if Linda sold it well, she would. And Karen knew when to call them. Reading hitters was an art she'd mastered. She communicated the next pitch to Linda in a series of complicated hand signs the two of them had developed with Coach.

Karen made the call and I bit back a smile. I loved this move. Linda nodded, ready to throw her signature heat. Throw after throw had gone screaming past the plate. The batter tightened up her grip and moved back in the box in preparation for the next pitch, angling for some extra time to watch the ball.

Linda paused, building anticipation. When she was ready, she wound up and released. The batter heaved a mighty swing. But clever Linda only made it look like she was throwing a fastball. Instead, the ball rolled off her fingers, floating past the plate and dipping gently into Karen's outstretched glove.

Off-speed. The most deadly pitch in Linda's arsenal. The hitter never saw it coming and always ended up looking like a damn fool.

The force of the girl's swing sent her spinning around as the bat sliced through the air without resistance.

"Stee-rike three. You're outta there," the ump said.

The girl stomped off, face burning. I pitied her. A spectator would think she'd completely whiffed it. But at the plate, you only got a second to decide if you were going to swing or not. If it looked like it was coming in good, you had to go for it. But Linda always made it look like it was coming in good. That's why she was the best. No shame in getting beat out by that. That's what made this game so interesting. Brawn would only get you so far in softball. You needed brains out there.

Thanks to Linda, we managed to completely shut down their offence. But their defense was nothing to sneeze at. Play after play got snuffed by their killer infield. The outfield were no slouches either. I got robbed of at least a double by the center fielder's incredible diving catch in the fifth that left grass stains all up the front of her uniform. I kicked up the dirt by first in frustration, but I got enough of a grip on myself to tip my batting helmet to her in appreciation. It really was a hell of a catch.

"Nice hit," Jem said when I got back to the dugout.

I narrowed my eyes, bracing for sarcasm, but he was earnest.

"Bad luck about the catch, but you're on to them now."

"Thanks," I replied.

The game was still scoreless by the bottom of the sixth and we were getting restless. Jane had managed to get on base, but that was it. Two were away and I was up.

Coach ambled over to me in the on-deck circle. No matter how tense the game, he always acted like we were just having a friendly practice. His steady directions never betrayed an ounce of stress.

"This is it, kid. We end this game right now. You get Jane home and we'll take care of the rest. You hear me?"

I nodded.

"Good," he said and gave me a too-hard pat on the top of my helmet. He liked to do it to rattle the yips out.

I exhaled and walked up to the plate. The outfield took a few steps back as the pitcher readied. They respected me. I liked that.

Now, there were two schools of thought on whether or not you should swing on the first pitch. Some people thought it was a disaster. They said that you were more likely to pop off on some garbage throw. That it was better to wait her out. Sit on the plate and force her to pitch you the throw you wanted. See what she's got, get in her head, and make her work for every strike. Those who disagreed said if the pitch is your pitch, you gotta swing no matter what order it was coming in. It was silly to waste a perfect throw on a dumb rule like never swinging on the first pitch.

I tended to side with those people. Besides, I'd already seen what number 17 had all game. And I knew she was getting tired. Pitches were getting a little slower. And they were starting to come in dead on or way off. I knew she was going to toss the first one out as well as she could.

I locked eyes with her. Sweat dripped down her forehead as she readied on the mound. Her body leaned slightly back before she snapped back her arm and released.

I never blinked.

The ball came in hard and true. The bat sang as it connected right on the sweet spot. My heart in my throat, I started to run without seeing where it landed. I knew in my bones it was good. Coach told me later that it sailed right past the center fielder's head and over the fence.

I heard roaring in my ears as I circled the bases. It wasn't the crowd. It was the blood pouring to my head, my heart pounding in my ears. I thought my chest would explode with joy as I touched home plate.

Tears sprang to my eyes as my teammates smothered me with screams and hugs. We still had work to do, but everyone knew it was over. We could see it in the way the Spartans hunched their shoulders. Silly. In baseball, it's not over until the last out, but the Spartans were already acting like they were beat.

Linda had two out and one on first when the last batter of the game stepped to the plate. Linda tossed it low and outside and the hitter just got a piece of it, sending it dribbling my way. Just a routine play, I told myself. No need to panic. I calmly snagged the ball, sending a gentle toss to Cher. She double-checked her foot was on the bag and caught the ball neatly. Out.

We had just won the state championship. I had just won the state championship.

The tears that started with my hit came in earnest now. The baseball diamond was my true home. I lived for the hot sun on my neck and ballpark dust in my lungs. When I stepped out on that dirt I wasn't the Bliss that Mama and Daddy wanted me to be. I wasn't Michael's girlfriend, or Bliss Bennet the debutante. I was just me, doing something that I loved. Not only that, I was good at it. How many people were lucky enough to be good — scratch that — great at what they loved?

Hitting that home run was the greatest moment of my life. Which made it hurt even worse. Because without some kind of miracle, I had just hit the last run of my softball career.

Chapter 4

My ears rang from all the screaming on the bus by the time we made it back to the school. Even Jem managed to crack a smile or two. Maybe the win had made me generous, but when Jem smiled I understood why some girls thought he was handsome.

"The club is going to have a reception for us," Nancy announced.

We cheered in response. Even though Peggy, Nancy and I were the only members of Uplands, nearly everyone had been there to use the pool at one point. Only Linda and Cher were less than thrilled.

Neither one of them fell into the ideal member category. Linda was Hispanic, so that was pretty much an automatic blackball. And Cher's father actually worked in the steel mill instead of being a company executive. Her mother did our mothers' hair. Our parents didn't like to sit down for meals with people who worked for them. They knew too many secrets.

I didn't understand the big deal. Cher and Linda's families were perfectly nice people. But it's not like they made enough money to pay the club fees anyway. I'm not sure what admitting them would change. The club was for people who could afford it and they couldn't. That was just the way the cookie crumbled. Life wasn't fair and we all had our roles to play.

Nancy was holding court with a group of girls, describing her dress for the debutante ball in excruciating detail.

"We're getting it from Saks in New York and I'm flying there for the final fitting next month," she said. "It's impossible to get anything of the same quality here. Even in the city."

She gave me a smug look. "Where's your dress from, Bliss?"

"Um, it's also from out-of-town," I replied. Trust Nancy to compete over dumb stuff. If it wasn't baseball, I didn't get the point. "I let Mama take care of the details."

"Sure," Nancy said. "Well, you'll have to make sure to let me see the label when you wear it."

Peggy knew exactly what Nancy was getting at, but she widened her big eyes with fake innocence.

"You didn't hear?" She asked.

Nancy pursed her lips. "It can't be that exciting since Bliss won't talk about it."

Peggy smiled coyly.

"Bliss's dress is coming from Paris!" She continued. "You know Mrs. Bennet used to model when she was young. She kept all her old contacts. Bliss is getting a custom-made Chanel gown. It's absolutely fab."

Nancy's cheeks bloomed two hot pinpricks of red.

"Well isn't that exciting," she said like she'd just swallowed mud.

"Isn't it, just?" Peggy asked, sweet as mud pie.

I wanted her to give it a break. As my best friend, Peggy was my sworn defender against the snubs of Nancy Bell. But it was painful to rub Nancy's nose in something I didn't even care about. We needed a change of topic.

"Peggy, I thought you said you had a veil you wanted to show me?"

It was all the encouragement Peggy needed to pull out her latest copy of Brides magazine with its many dog-eared pages. She meticulously outlined the pros and cons of each style until the bus pulled into the school parking lot and a cluster of noise got our attention.

"A welcoming committee!" Peggy said, pointing out a crowd of students holding congratulatory signs.

Right in the middle with the largest sign and the biggest smile was George. What would it feel like to have someone who was that proud of my game?

I scanned the crowd for Michael. He was waiting for me, leaned up against his silver Mercedes. Nancy gave him an up and down, noting his slick internship suit. He was spending summer break working for his father's steel company.

"Princeton suits him," Nancy said appreciatively.

I smiled at the note of jealousy in her voice, proud that Michael was waiting for me. The navy suit brought out the blue in his eyes. His cut marble face glowed in the setting sun. He was the most beautiful man I had ever seen and I knew I wasn't the only one who thought so. A number of girls in the waiting crowd checked him out. Michael was from town but had gone to boarding school, so he was an unfamiliar face. He was gorgeous, successful, rich, and he was mine. I shivered in pleasure. Eat it up, ladies. I was the undisputed national champion of the boyfriend game.

"Michael," I said, running to him the moment the bus doors opened.

He gave me a deep, slow kiss. The kind that made my stomach tingle and my mind forget the final score.

"How did it go?" He asked.

"We won! We're the state champions!" I was jumping out of my skin with excitement.

Michael's response was measured.

"Hey, that's far out, babe. But I should get you back home, ASAP. Your mother is all worked up, and your father is worked up that your mother's worked up. The sooner you walk through the front door and get cleaned up the better."

I wanted to tell him all about my home run and about Linda's masterful pitching. The words bubbled in my throat, but Michael was focused on getting me in the car. He opened the passenger door and held it for me, closing it gently as I settled into the leather seat.

He got behind the wheel.

"Let me tell ya, I had a hell of a day today," he said. "These imports are just killing us."

"Oh, really?" I asked.

Maybe a stressful day wasn't the time to brag about my accomplishments.

Michael's face lit up when he talked about steel and his family's business. I tried my best to seem interested as we pulled out, but instead, I kept replaying the game in my head, trying to hold onto that warm feeling of victory.

As we turned onto the street, Jem came running up at full speed and knocked on my window. Michael jumped, recovered, and then leaned over to roll down my window.

"Watch it, man," he said to Jem. "I just had the car detailed."

"What is it?" I asked Jem, annoyance battled with eagerness to not let go of my perfect afternoon just yet.

"Coach needs to see you in his office," Jem said. He wasn't even out of breath from his sprint.

"Can't it wait?" Michael said. "Bliss really needs to get home."

"Coach said to get you," Jem replied, directing his answer to me. "He said it's important."

"Alright, she's coming. Tell him she'll be along in a second," Michael said in the imperious voice he saved for waiters at the club.

Jem jogged back to the gym office.

"Poor son of a bitch," Michael said, watching his retreating back.

"Hey, coaching us isn't that bad," I said, defensive.

"For Jem, I think it might be."

Michael's comment grated as I walked to Coach's office. Stupid, stuck-up Jem. We were state champions. Could the boys' baseball team say as much? Hell, they hadn't even made playoffs this year. And if it weren't for Jem, they probably wouldn't have won a single game.

Coach was on the phone when I got to his office with the familiar smell of gym socks and cleaning solutions. Trophies lined the shelves and photos of smiling teams past gathered dust on the walls. Coach was crazy about the Indians. Bobbleheads decorated his desk. Pennants and posters filled the wall space. A signed baseball held the place of honor next to his lamp.

"Great news, Jerry. I'll let her know. Thanks again."

Coach hung up and beamed at me. He rubbed his hands together with glee.

"Listen, kid, don't let anyone ever tell ya that your Congress does nothing for you. Thanks to Title IX, colleges can't get enough quality girls out there playing for them," he said.

"What does that have to do with me?" I asked.

I didn't really pay much attention when Title IX got passed last year. All I knew is that it was a law that forced schools that received federal funding for sports to provide equal opportunities for men and women. I only gleaned that much because Daddy was hopping mad that the government had butt in on how schools did business. He swore at the newspaper every morning that year. Mama thought it was undignified that any woman should be playing sports past childhood. For her, college was about further refinement and social opportunity. She hadn't even bothered to ask me what I wanted to study at Bryn Mawr. To her, it was beside the point.

"Get your head in the game, Bennet! It has everything to do with you. That was just Arizona State on the phone."

I held my breath. Once more, the blood rushed in my ears.

"They want you! They're prepared to offer you a full scholarship to play softball for them. And you know they're the best team in the country, two years in a row. Their shortstop is a senior, and they want to groom you as her replacement. You report to training camp on August 6th."

The Monday after the deb ball.

Disbelief shocked me into a state of blankness. I had been given a chance to keep playing softball on a silver platter. Like a genie just popped out of a bottle and granted my secret heart's desire without me saying a single word.

"You have anything to say for yourself?" Coach asked.

"I, I can't believe it," I said, stunned.

"Well, snap out of it, cause it's true. C'mere."

Coach shuffled out from behind his desk, eyes twinkling as he wrapped me in a gruff hug. I rested in it, letting the feeling return to my body and give way to joy.

"Your parents are going to be so proud of you. Want to give them a call now?" Coach asked.

And my happy bubble burst. Oh, how wrong Coach was. Nothing about this news would make Mama and Daddy happy.

"No," I replied. "I'll tell them in person." After I work up the nerve to do it.

"Alright then," Coach said, giving me a gruff pat on the back. "You tell that hotshot boyfriend of yours to get you home in good time, you hear?"

I nodded. There was no problem with that. Michael would make like a bat out of hell if he thought that would make Daddy happy.

"Nice work kid, I'm proud of you."

I returned his smile sadly. The end of my high school career also meant the end of chats with Coach. His style was abrupt, but he was always there when I needed him. His presence in my life had been more steady than Mama and Daddy's over the past four years.

"Thanks, Coach," I said, pausing at the door of his office before leaving him behind.

"What was so important?" Michael asked when I got back to the car.

I opened my mouth to tell him and shut it again. I wasn't ready to hear all the reasons it would never work out. How my parents would never let me go, how I already had college plans and they had nothing to do with Arizona. If I never mentioned my dream out loud, I could hold onto it for a little longer.

"Nothing," I replied.

Chapter 5

There was no celebratory dinner at home that night. Mama quivered on the chaise-lounge in her dressing gown while Daddy gave me a dressing down.

They had a cocktail party to get to. Mama's lovely copper hair was done up in big curlers, her big green eyes fringed with her longest fake lashes. Daddy, of course, had been ready to go for ages. His cufflinks and freshly polished shoes shone. Between Mama's hair and her feathered robe, she looked like a big red tropical bird. I bit back a laugh when she spoke. One glare from Daddy made me zip it.

His dark eyes flashed, his moustache quivered. His voice stayed dangerously calm. I braced for what was to come.

"Young lady, you frightened your mother half to death. What do you have to say for yourself?" Daddy asked.

"Sorry, Mama," I said.

"That's it?" Daddy demanded.

"I'm sorry, Mama. It was wrong for me to sneak out of Mrs. Popple's class like that."

I tried to act contrite. The truth was, I wasn't sorry at all.

"And to give me such a fright! Sugar, I didn't know if you had keeled over in a ditch somewhere. And all that trouble for what? To play a game? Look at you, you're positively filthy. You're covered in dirt. And your nails! You know how long it took them to fix at the salon last time. Let me see them."

Wincing, I stepped forward and let Mama inspect my manicure. I already knew what she would see: the watermelon polish was chipped and peeling, and I had broken at least one nail. There was dirt jammed down into my cuticles and blisters on my fingertips. Signs of a game well-played, but to Mama, it just meant I was being careless with my appearance.

"These are not the hands of a lady, Bliss. Goodness, the girls at the salon are going to have a heck of a time trying to put your nails back in order. I'll make an appointment tomorrow."

I sucked back annoyance and held my hands behind my back. I had to remember that I was lucky to be so pampered. Cher's hands were chapped raw from washing hair at the salon. It was how she saved the money for her prom dress. Mama took me to Barney's for mine, flashing Daddy's American Express card.

"Sorry, Mama," I said. Maybe if I kept saying sorry enough they would just leave me alone to savour my win and dream my impossible dream of playing forever.

"Well thank goodness we're done with softball. Now you won't be tracking mud into the house anymore. It's impossible for Rosa to clean up, you know," Mama said.

Not that she actually gave a hoot what was hard or not for our maid to deal with.

Daddy sighed with impatience.

"Marie, now that we've dealt with the important issue of grooming, let us turn to our daughter's defiance. Lying and sneaking out are unacceptable, young lady. I knew we should have sent you to prep school. We didn't let you play on that little team of yours so you could run around deceiving us."

My cheeks flushed with shame. I prided myself on being a straight shooter, but Daddy was right. I was no better than a liar.

"I know," I said. I should have done better. But what choice did I really have?

"Well understand this, you are on probation until the Cotillion ball. That means you will go straight to your deb class and any other cotillion events and then straight home," Daddy said.

"But I have a — " I started.

"Don't worry," Mama soothed, interrupting me. "You can still go out and see Michael. We know you have a date tomorrow."

I was going to say I had to go to my softball party, but it didn't matter. I could always get Michael to take me if I was still allowed to see him.

Daddy frowned, seeming to weigh the pros and cons of letting me go out with my boyfriend. It wasn't a long debate. He practically thought Michael walked on water, the son he wished he'd had. Daddy wouldn't want to cause a rift in our relationship.

"You can see Michael as long as it doesn't interfere with any of your other activities. Your mother hasn't forgotten the deal you struck with her. There will be an etiquette refresher course. Attendance is mandatory," Daddy said.

Argh, more nonsense about cutlery and courtesy to take up brain space.

"Yes, Daddy," I mumbled.

"That's enough attitude, Bliss," Daddy said. "I just hope this was a one-time incident and not part of a larger pattern."

What he meant was: I hope you're not turning out like Kathleen.

"This was a one-off, I promise."

What I meant was: No, of course, I'm not like her.

Daddy nodded and gave me a pat on the head like I was his favorite retriever. He wasn't one for a lot of affection. Mama, on the other hand, swooped in for a big kiss, enveloping me in her powdery cloud of perfume.

"Darling, go to the kitchen and get yourself something to eat. I've had Rosa make up a salad for you. You're starting to get a little hippy," she said.

I gritted my teeth. Mama was constantly on me to watch the size of my thighs. Maybe they were bigger than Jane Seymour's, but that was because they were muscular. I needed that power to race down the baseline. But I guess I didn't need to be fast anymore. Better start getting used to salads.

Daddy checked his watch. "Marie, I'd like to make it to this event sometime this decade. Do you think you could hurry up your preparations?"

Mama waved him off. She took forever to get ready, but the result was always worth the wait. Just like a real lady.

Chapter 6

The phone rang while I was getting ready for my date with Michael. Daddy was still at the office and Mama was having a lie-down, so I rushed to the hallway to answer it, my dress tangled over my head.

"Bennet?"

Oh, shoot. I should have had Rosa answer.

"Hi Coach," I said, sheepishly. He was calling about the Arizona scholarship and I still hadn't figured out a way to tell him that I couldn't take it. I racked my brain for a good stall tactic.

"Yeah, yeah," Coach said, not listening to me. "That's not what I called to talk about."

"It's not?" Then I was confused. The season was over and we had nothing else to discuss.

"Nope. I'm just calling to tell you to keep up whatever post-season juju you've had going on."

He'd lost me. What on earth was he talking about?

"But softball is done. Isn't it?" I asked.

"I can't get into all the details yet, but we've been tapped to play a tournament. The first of its kind. Very hush-hush, lots of pressure. You think we can handle it?"

Handle it? Of course, I could handle it! My heart thrilled. I wasn't done yet. I still had a chance to play!

"You know we can," I said.

"Good, that's what I want to hear from you, Bennet," Coach said. "Now, you'll get all the details later, but for now, just keep doing that weird stuff you've been doing. I'm not a superstitious man myself, but hell, you need to respect the streak."

The streak! Shit! Panicked, my mind raced. Where were my socks? Oh crap, they hadn't been washed, had they? Still tangled in my dress, I sprinted to the laundry room. Rosa hadn't sorted my things yet. Tossing clothes aside, I fished my lucky knee socks out of the hamper. Yeah, they were rancid but there was no washing them until this tournament was over. I held them away from the silk of my dress. I didn't want the smell rubbing off.

Right, socks were secure. I would figure out how to deal with the parents later.

When I was untangled and ready for my date, Mama roused and gave me an approving once over. Michael was taking me out to some fancy restaurant, and I had opted for an emerald green halter maxi dress and a pair of black suede platform sandals. Mama brushed out my hair, the same copper penny color as her own, and hummed.

"Aren't you just a vision? My little darling. Michael is going to be so proud he's your beau."

I smiled. I loved when Mama came out of her room and was in a good mood. It was becoming rarer and rarer these days. The music stopped and she sprung up to put a new record on, her favourite Frank Sinatra.

Daddy walked into the living room and Mama grabbed his hands for a dance. Daddy and I exchanged wary glances. It was also possible for Mama to be in too good of a mood.

"Chip, honey! Look at our beautiful daughter," Mama said.

Daddy softened. "Just like you at that age," he said, his eyes far away. He turned stern with me.

"You make sure Michael gets you home at a decent hour. I don't care how beautiful you are," he said.

"Yes, Daddy."

On cue, the doorbell rang.

"Oh, he's here!" Mama squealed as if Michael hadn't already been over countless times before. We'd been going steady for a whole year. He had stopped by the house plenty of times.

"Evening, Mr. and Mrs. Bennet," Michael said after Rosa showed him in. "Thank you for letting me take Bliss out tonight. I know she's mostly grounded."

Mama gushed all over Michael until we could escape. I felt like I would burst out of my skin waiting until we were alone to share my good news about our tournament.

"Guess what?" I said as I settled until the plush leather seat of Michael's car. I didn't wait for him to guess. "Coach called today. The Lady Scarlets are going to play in some big tournament!"

I could hardly believe I was speaking the words, I was so excited.

"Are you sure your parents are going to go for that?" Michael asked, concern etched on his face.

My smile dimmed. Not exactly the reaction I was hoping for. He had a point, but I wasn't ready to hear it. I wanted to stay in my happy bubble of excitement for a little bit first. I decided to not mention Arizona either. I didn't want cold reality anywhere near that either yet.

"I hope they'll let me play," I said, realizing now that I actually had no idea if they would or not.

"It's just that they seemed pretty angry about you sneaking out of deb class last night. I think if softball weren't over for the season they would have gone a bit harder on you. Jim at my office has a son who's playing in a tournament coming up. They're going to New York City if you can believe it. From the sounds of it, they're doing more sightseeing than they are playing. Jim's taking a week off to go with them, which is leaving us all short-staffed. I mean, the man has projects he's in the middle of. Father says if you can just up and leave, it shows that you're not that essential. But the good news is that he's going to let me take on some of Jim's duties while he's away..."

And on Michael went. Just like that, he had brought my tournament around to his favorite topic: work. Mama said it was a lady's job to love and support her husband, and always listen to what was on his mind. If Michael wanted to talk about work instead of softball, it meant that my tournament was nothing to worry about. The last thing I wanted to do was bore him, so I easily went along with the change of subject. I'd hate to come across as one of those "me-first" girls Michael was always complaining about. I settled back into my headrest and tried to get my distracted mind to focus on his words until it was obvious that we weren't driving into town. We had veered into farm country, with bright green pastures all around.

"Where are we?" I asked as we pulled down a dirt road.

"Hanlon Farm, owned by my mother's cousin. They're away this week and I thought we might have a picnic in the orchards."

I flushed. This was exactly the type of romantic gesture at which Michael excelled. He pulled a basket of food and a woollen blanket from his trunk.

"Follow me," he said, taking me gently by the hand.

The last of the fluffy white blooms still clung to the branches of the apple tree. They smelled sticky sweet. Michael set us up underneath the tree and produced a bottle of champagne.

"What is this for?" I asked.

"For the next step in your life. Bryn Mawr and whatever comes after..."

The cork popped and champagne burst out the top. I giggled as Michael tried to corral the fountain of fizz into the glasses.

"Cheers," he said, clinking his flute to mine.

I nibbled on my sandwich and sipped slowly while I watched Michael inhale his food. I didn't want him to think I was a heifer by eating so fast. When he was done, he refilled my glass. My head was as bubbly as the champagne.

"It's so beautiful here," I said, my words slightly slurred. "Thank you for bringing me."

Who else had a gorgeous Princeton boyfriend who took her on romantic picnics in apple orchards? Nancy Bell would be green with envy if she saw me right now.

Michael took the champagne flute from my hand and set it down.

"Show me how thankful you are," he said.

He kissed me, a hot crushing kiss as I brought my hands around his neck. He pushed me down against the blanket and I shivered as he ran his hands along my shoulders, down over my breasts. I could feel the heat spreading through me as our kisses grew deeper.

"Oh Bliss," Michael said, his breath hot in my ear.

He took my hand and led it down to cup him.

"This is what you do to me," he said.

Mama had told me I better do everything in my power to save my flower for marriage. No one wanted to buy the cow when the milk was free. So far, I had resisted. But George and Peggy had done it and they were getting married. Then again, so had Kathleen and she definitely wasn't. Michael wanted to and I wanted him. When he kissed me, I forgot myself. I forgot all my dreams.

Michael grabbed a rubber from his jacket pocket.

"Do you want to?" He asked.

From somewhere deep inside me, a strange voice I didn't recognize as my own answered.

"No," I said.

Michael moaned and flopped onto his back. Oh, maybe I should. I was going to make him so mad.

"Bliss! Come on. You're going to give me blue balls," he said, a whiny edge to his plea.

The voice again: "No. I can't. I'm sorry."

I wanted to have sex with Michael. Wanted to desperately. It was the power of my wanting that scared me. I was afraid of the power Michael would have over me if I gave in.

Chapter 7

ven though I was grounded after the championship game, Mama still let me go to Peggy's house on Friday night for my dress fitting. With Mama, being grounded basically meant I was only allowed to do the things Mama approved of.

At Peggy's, I sunk into the soft orange shag carpeting in the living room and used the floral patterned ottoman as a desk to write out the endless invitations, a duty that unfortunately fell to me, her maid of honor. When I complained that my hands were cramping, Peggy just kissed me on the cheek.

"Don't worry, one day I'll return the favor for you. That's how it works! And between you and Michael, you'll probably have twice as many guests. Then I'll be sorry," she said.

"Who says I'm marrying Michael?" I asked with pleasure.

Peggy gave me her best, 'please don't play dumb with me, Bliss Bennet,' look as she picked lint off the sleeve of her white peasant top.

"Fine," I said, unable to stop a goofy grin from spreading across my face. "But not anytime soon. And make it three times the guests. With a bridesmaid's dress that's twice as ugly."

Peggy mock gasped. "Are you saying the lovely dress that George's mother has picked for you is ugly? Why I never."

We giggled. The bridesmaids were being forced into a green crinoline explosion gave us all seasick cast. Mama thought they were sweet.

"What are you girls laughing about?" Mrs. Harmon asked, bringing us each a sweating glass of Tang.

"Nothing!" We chorused.

Even with the wedding four months out, all of the women in George and Peggy's extended family were crammed into the Harmon' living room for fittings. The blessed day would have six bridesmaids, three junior bridesmaids, four flower girls, two ring bearers and assorted ushers. Plus, the mothers of the bride and groom needed special dresses made. The stressed seamstress barked measurements to her assistant, who dutifully recorded them.

Peggy's house was the complete opposite of mine and I loved it. Instead of austere coldness, the Harmons' house was always too hot, too full, and lots of fun. Assorted grandmothers pressed food on everyone, babies crawled across the floor or cried in their mothers' laps. Swatches of fabric and stationery were scattered haphazardly throughout the room. And in the middle of it all, sat Peggy, beatific. She wore her veil to get herself into the wedding mood. It wasn't the ideal place to confide in my best friend, but it was the first chance I'd had to talk to her since Coach's mysterious phone call so we could speculate on the tournament.

"Who do you think we're going to play?" I asked. "Probably some hotshot team from out west. California, maybe."

"What?" Peggy asked, distracted by her mother's lace selection.

"The top-secret tournament!" I said. "Why won't they tell us who it is? Maybe they have to lock down all the details first. I hope it's out of town. Won't it be so fun to bunk together? Like when we were at camp."

That's when we first made friends. Peggy stood up for me when a posse of girls said only boys liked sports. At the end of the week, Daddy and Mama came to pick me up in the Jaguar and those same girls tried to act nice so they could get up close. Only Peggy got a ride.

"Right, honey, the thing about that tournament is..." Peggy said

I took in the chaos around her and my stomach sank. Oh, right. Peggy had bigger fish to fry these days.

"You can't play, can you?"

She shook her head. "Not with all of this going on. I can't let Mom steamroll the planning or George's mother will get upset. And we have a lot of work to do to the backyard still for the reception. And we have all of our deb classes. I love playing softball, but I was relieved the season was over. It frees up my time for other things." She shrugged.

I swallowed hard, trying to push down my disappointment. I would give anything to play softball every single day. And here was the perfect chance to just play a little longer! Couldn't Peggy see that this stuff wasn't as important as what happened out on the diamond?

"I don't understand," I said finally, feeling the corners of my mouth turning downward.

Peggy patted my cheek. "I know how important softball is to you. But to me, it's just a game. This is my life," she said, sweeping her arm around the room. "And I want to get it started right away. Maybe one day you'll feel the same way."

I fought back tears. I mean, I obviously was going to get married. But what did that have to do with giving up softball?

"I just -" I said, but we were interrupted by shrieking from the younger cousins.

"George is here! George is here! Peggy, take your veil off! Cover the measurements! It's bad luck for him to see anything!"

Grateful for the distraction, I scooped the veil off Peggy's head and tucked it behind my cushion.

George crept in, bashful.

"I just wanted to see how my girl was doing," he said, leaning down for a kiss. "Now I'm sorry I interrupted."

There was a chorus of squeals as George tugged one of Peggy's honey-colored curls. It was still incredible that George had managed to snag Peggy. Peggy could be a Bond girl. George on the other hand, with his stocky build, longish nose and ginger coloring was not what you would call traditionally handsome. But he was kind and he made Peggy laugh like no one else could.

When they first started to date, I asked Peggy if she thought George was a little, you know.

"What?" She had asked.

"You know, not as foxy as you," I said in the most diplomatic way possible.

"He isn't? I think he's just dreamy," she said.

Love is blind, as Mama would say.

George teased Peggy by trying to peek at the fabric swatches. She squealed and swatted him away. And then they started an earnest discussion about the barn in the back of George's family property they were converting into their new home.

I sat back, content to watch true love in progress. I understood why Peggy was willing to give up softball. She had her dream wedding to plan with her big, happy family. I wanted this too, eventually. I wanted a big church wedding in a white dress with a long train and a big bouquet of peonies. With Michael, I could have all that.

I didn't ask Peggy if she was getting married now because she didn't want to wait to start her life or if George wouldn't wait for her. The googly eyes they were always giving each other answered my question. I wondered if Peggy thought it was possible to go away to Arizona for four years and then come back and get married. Would Michael wait for me? I thought guiltily of refusing his advances on our last date. Michael wasn't really the waiting kind.

Chapter 8

It was late when I got home from Peggy's, and no one had left the porch light on for me. Groping through the darkness, I heard snatches of raised voices. Mama and Daddy were at it again, arguing about something.

They weren't always like this.

There was a time when Mama and Daddy were absolutely golden. Not long after Daddy met Mama at his frat brother's wedding in Charleston, South Carolina. The way she tells it, Daddy was a strapping Yankee doodle dandy that swept her off her feet and convinced her to leave all her friends and family behind and move to our small Ohio town to enjoy the fortunes of his steel inheritance.

Daddy didn't stay at the office as late as he did now and Mama didn't always take those pills that Dr. Nicholas prescribed. Before Rosa started doing the cleaning up, Mama was proud of the care she took of the house and of her girls.

My classmates were always jealous of the elaborate lunches she packed for us. Real country cooking, Mama said. While the other kids ate bologna on Wonder Bread, Kathleen and I feasted on sliced ham, fresh biscuits, corn, green beans and cold chicken. Mama would get up first thing in the morning and make a huge breakfast for all of us, making sure that the coffee was brewing for Daddy and the newspaper was waiting at his place. The table was always perfectly set with her willow pattern china, fresh flowers that Daddy had brought home for her sitting in a pretty vase in the middle. Mama would be waiting for us, fully dressed, her hair in a neat bouffant, her face made up, her lipstick flawless. And when school was over, she'd have little snacks ready for us to munch while we did our homework.

While we'd been out for the day, she'd have been running around, doing a million little things. Mama was forever dropping clothes off at the cleaners or picking something up from the grocery, or buying craft supplies for our latest school project, or driving into town to check out the latest makeup collection. She volunteered as the church's fundraiser and read books to the residents at the old folks' home.

That was just during the day. At night, Mama and Daddy had plans nearly every evening. Cocktail parties, benefits, the orchestra, corporate events. Daddy kept her in an endless supply of velvet, silk, and crinoline dresses the colours of jewels, each one more beautiful than the next. He was so proud to have her on his arm. Daddy surprised her with jewelry. He said that a beautiful woman should have beautiful things. He also told us that Mama was his queen and that we should only ever date boys who treated us like the princesses that we were if he were ever going to let us date, that is.

This was before Kathleen went wild. After that, everyone would have loved to have seen her with a boyfriend who treated her halfway decent, nevermind like a princess.

Peggy's mother called Mama Superwoman because she managed to do three times as much as all the mothers at school and look twice as good doing it. I loved that. I wanted to be just like Mama. I wanted to be a Superwoman too. All the moms copied her hair and all the dads were always really polite to her and would stop to chat like they had all the time in the world to ask about her garden or how she thought the weather was going to turn out that weekend. She would laugh and tease them about anything, her musical southern accent making every word a song.

Then one day Mama slept in. Daddy thought she must have been sick. He scrambled to put breakfast together for us. Then Mama slept in the day after. And the day after that. Pretty soon she just stopped getting out of bed. Not even to make dinner. There were no more after school snacks. Rosa started coming to the house and Mama visited Dr. Nicholas for the first time. Daddy worked late.

Mama eventually got out of bed, but we were forbidden from ever talking about it. If we were lucky, her episodes only happened once a year. But there were triggers. Like when Kathleen ran off and she went into her room for a month. She made me promise I would never abandon the family like that. Daddy told everyone Mama had appendicitis. It was what she would have wanted.

Because even when she was in bed and her little girls' stomachs were growling because no one packed them lunch, Mama still cared about what people thought. No one was perfect, but it was important to give that impression. That was why she and Daddy still went out, even if her heart wasn't in it. Even if Daddy didn't call her his queen anymore or buy her jewelry. Even if Rosa made my lunch now. The Bennet family policy was that we were all a-ok. Thriving even, thank you very much for asking, and how were you finding the weather? Hot enough for you?

I remembered that when I thought about Arizona. Mama would have a hell of a time explaining why I wasn't going to Bryn Mawr, and she'd be none too pleased about it.

"I won't stand for it! This is completely unacceptable," Daddy yelled.

I blanched. Oh God, he'd found out about the softball tournament from Coach before I'd had a chance to lay my groundwork. If he was already dead set against it, I'd have no chance of playing.

"Chip, please! Wait!"

Mama sobbed.

I tried to sneak as quietly as possible up the stairs to my bedroom, avoiding the sliver of light from the opening in Mama and Daddy's door. Yelling was something new for them. They'd been doing it a lot lately and it was unsettling change from the usual icy silence.

Distracted by approaching footsteps, I tripped over a vase in the hallway and fell into the wall. A family portrait taken when Kathleen and I were girls fell and the glass shattered. Shards ricocheted throughout the hallway. My heart thumped with every falling piece of glass.

Daddy wrenched open the bedroom door. His tie was askew, his eyes red and bleary. I could smell the drink on him. I froze like I was standing at the plate, watching a bad hit pop up and waiting for the inevitable out.

Daddy peered at me, his eyes focussed and unfocused.

"Kathleen?"

Oh lord, he was really gone.

"No Daddy, it's Bliss," I said, voice quavering.

"Kathleen, we've all missed you," he said.

I put my hand on his arm. "Daddy. Kathleen isn't here. It's Bliss."

He shook me off, baring his teeth like an animal.

"What the fuck are you looking at?"

My entire body shook in fear and disgust. I wanted to flee, but my legs were useless and rooted to the floor. I had never, ever heard Daddy use the f-word like that. And the sharp dagger of the word was directed at me. No one had ever spoken to me like that before, never mind my own father. I was supposed to be his princess. I didn't even recognize the man swearing at me.

In the hallway, there was only the sound of his harsh breathing.

"Daddy-" I cried out, my voice ragged with tears. I reached toward him, but he pushed past me and stumbled down the stairs.

I was still frozen in place when Mama came into the hallway. I sobbed in earnest and tried to hug her, seeking comfort. Instead, she brushed my arms aside.

"Go to bed, Bliss," she said, and went back into her room, slamming the door behind her.

Alone in the dark again, I sank to the floor, crying in loud, gasping sobs. I'm here too, I wanted to scream. I was a person with real hopes and dreams, not just an accessory to the perfect family! From the outside, my life was wonderful. But the price of all of those perks meant quietly going along with the plan, no matter what. It was all a huge lie and I was tired of living it.

Cried out, I pulled myself up and staggered to my room. I needed to figure out a way to get to Arizona.

Chapter 9

The house was quiet the day after Daddy cursed at me in the hallway. He must have gone into the office and Mama had surely cocooned herself in bed for the day. Someone had cleaned up the glass already. It couldn't have been Rosa, who wasn't due until later in the afternoon.

"Mama?" I called into the crack of her door.

No answer. I tried again, a little louder.

"Mama?"

Silence. No one could accuse me of not trying to get permission to go out today.

In the kitchen, I grabbed toast and the keys to Mama's Volvo. I'd be back before she knew they were gone. If this trip went well, I'd be on my way to Arizona in the fall.

It was an hour's drive to Lakewood to visit my Aunt Cordelia. She wasn't really my aunt, but one of the many women from her sorority days who Mama called sister. I got the impression that the two of them hadn't been the closest in college, but geographical coincidence had thrown them together. Southern girls adrift in Ohio needed to stick together and Mama and Aunt Cordelia were thick as thieves. Or at least they had been. We haven't had Aunt Cordelia round that often lately.

I pulled into the driveway of Aunt Cordelia's oversized home. It was quiet. I should have called before coming. But I banked on the fact that Cordelia wasn't out much these days.

I rang the doorbell. No answer. I tried again, knocking this time. Finally, heavy footsteps paired with mild cursing approached the entrance.

"What?" Aunt Cordelia said, ripping open the door.

I tried to smile, but I couldn't hide my shock. The Aunt Cordelia I knew didn't pick the newspaper off the front stoop without a full face of makeup. Yet here she was, face undid, greasy blonde hair showing two inches of roots, and still in her fraying silk bathrobe.

"Aunt Cordelia?"

Instantly she brightened.

"Oh, Bliss! I'm sorry darling, I thought it was one of those awful neighbor boys banging on the door. I wasn't expecting to see you!"

She held me in a warm hug and I caught traces of Chanel No. 5. At least that was the same.

"Come in, come in, dearest."

Aunt Cordelia led me through the grand marble foyer, past a perfect rectangle of yellow paint two shades darker than the rest of the wall where the giant portrait of her and her husband used to hang. Wilted flowers had been left in a vase to drop dried petals all over the floor.

Aunt Cordelia usually liked to be as turned out as Mama. She was off her game today.

"Is everything okay?" I asked, bracing for her answer.

"Oh sure, Sugar. Please excuse the state of things. I just haven't had that many visitors lately. You'd think I was contagious. Hello, I'm not the one who ran off with my 22-year-old secretary. Richard is the one who's sick, not me!"

I wasn't sure if I should laugh or not. I raised my eyebrows and murmured something non-committal.

"That was a joke, sweetheart!" Aunt Cordelia said, swatting my arm. Her normally flawless red nails were bitten down to stubs. "Lighten up! You want a drink?"

A drink? What planet was I on? Where was the etiquette obsessed southern Auntie I knew?

"Mama would flip," I said. Plus, it wasn't even noon.

Aunt Cordelia made herself a martini. The marabou trim of her robe shook as she mixed her drink. She puffed her cigarette and ash sprinkled on the Persian rug. I ran for an ashtray.

"Here, you're dropping cigarette everywhere," I said, trying to catch the falling ash.

"Sug, I am past the point of caring. Thanks to the infidelity clause of our prenup, I'm a millionaire. I wish I could see Richard's mother's face when she writes that check. I know she had that put in to keep me in line and now it's backfired all over her perfect son."

Aunt Cordelia cackled and took a swig of martini, made a face and added more gin. Mama had told me about the money. That's why I was here.

If this were a typical visit, Aunt Cordelia would be fussing with lemonade and snacks. Today she didn't seem to care if she offered the correct hospitality. Maybe that's what happened when you tried to be an ideal wife and ended up as a divorcee no one invited to dinner parties anymore. Even when you did everything right, you could still end up wrong.

"I'm selling this dump, furniture and all, first chance I get and moving back to Charleston," Aunt Cordelia said.

"We'll miss you," I replied.

Aunt Cordelia grabbed me under the chin and gave me a little shake. "You can come visit anytime you want, darlin'. I know your parents want you to go to one of those fancy Seven Sisters, but nothing beats a real down-home education."

"Speaking of college..." I started but was interrupted by the ringing phone.

"Hold on, I think that's the realtor now."

Aunt Cordelia scurried to the hallway and I stared at her sweating drink. After a heated phone conversation, she plunked down on the sofa.

"Tell me, how is your softball going, dear? Is that coach of yours as good-looking as ever?"

"Who, Jem?" I asked, incredulous. I thought about his soft brown eyes and his broad shoulders. And his permanent sneer. "I guess he's handsome if you like petulant men."

Aunt Cordelia was confused. "I thought his name was Wilfred."

Now I was confused. Did she mean Coach? He was old enough to be my father!

"Coach? Ew, no," I said.

"Let me guess sweetheart, any man over the age of 40 is ancient to you?"

I blushed because she was right.

"Now who is this Jem fellow? Does Michael have competition?"

Hoo boy. I could imagine Mama and Daddy's faces if I brought home a black boy. That was even more outside the realm of possibility than going to Arizona.

"Absolutely not," I said. "But, um, softball is going really well. Mama still isn't crazy about it, but we have this high-profile tournament coming up. I don't really have any of the details about it yet, but it's supposed to be a big deal."

"Well, I bet you're just going to shine. Make Marie come out and see you play. Prove to her how good you are and she won't be able to deny your talent," Cordelia said.

That was an idea I hadn't considered. Mama did love to show me off.

"You think so?" I asked.

"Honey, I know so. I've seen you play. You have a gift."

My cheeks flushed in excitement. This was the opportunity I'd been waiting for. If anyone knew how stupid it was to do exactly what was expected from you, surely Aunt Cordelia must. The whole story tumbled out. Arizona State, Bryn Mawr, sneaking out of deb class, getting grounded, how there was no way Mama and Daddy would let me go away.

"So maybe you could loan me a little money for my flight out west? Or even the bus. The scholarship takes care of everything else. I have a little saved for expenses. I just need to get there. And then once Mama and Daddy know they can't stop me from going, I'm sure they'll come around," I said, finished making my case.

Frowning, Aunt Cordelia aggressively stubbed out her cigarette. I held my breath. That wasn't exactly the reaction I'd banked on.

"It's out of the question. I couldn't possibly," she said.

"But, but..." I said looking around her opulent home. "It's not because you can't afford it, is it?"

"Bliss Bennet, this is a most uncivilized discussion! I will not help you go behind Chip and Marie's backs to run off to godforsaken Arizona. Your parents have thought this life through for you carefully. They know what's best and they want to make sure you get it."

My shoulders slouched. I'd just struck out big time.

"I thought you would understand," I said feebly. Now what was I supposed to do?

Aunt Cordelia touched my shoulder. Gin sloshed off the rim of her glass. Her eyes were tender, and even without makeup, it was obvious how beautiful she was.

"I do understand, Sugar. Better than you think. I thought Richard was my Arizona State. My parents warned me if I married him I would be a long way from home, that we weren't suited for each other. But oh no, I knew what I wanted. He was my dream. They raged and threatened and eventually begged me to stay. I didn't listen. And hoo boy, were they ever right, darling. So here I am, all alone, with all of this. And my dearest Daddy passed last year from a heart attack."

"I'm sorry," I said, contrite.

"Well, I'm sure your Mama has something to say about moving to Ohio for a man too. But the point I'm making is that your parents really do know what's best for you. They've had your whole life to think about it and plan for it. And whether you like it or not, they're the ones who know you best. They don't want you going across the country to run around outside like a heathen, they want you close to home at a proper school to grow up like the exceptional young lady that you are."

I bit my lip. Hot anger built up inside me until I couldn't contain it.

"I am exceptional! At the plate and at first, I am. I'm one of the best on my team, and the best team in the country wants me to come play for them. I can still be a lady and play softball, can't I?"

"I'm not sure about that, Sugar. But maybe if they see how good you are in this tournament, they'll encourage you to keep playing at Bryn Mawr."

Just like that, I deflated

"Bryn Mawr doesn't have a softball team."

Aunt Cordelia waved her hand dismissively and drained her glass.

"You're a smart girl. You'll find something else that holds your interest. But listen to your parents. Your place is close to home. Never forget that."

I left Aunt Cordelia's with a hardened resolve. I'd struck out, big time. But the game wasn't over. Her advice was useless to me. Just because things hadn't turned out for her, didn't mean that we were the same. She did give me a great idea. The odds were stacked against me for getting to Arizona, but I wasn't out yet. I still had another shot. If I played well and we won this tournament, Mama and Daddy would have to see that I was meant to go to Arizona. I would make them see.

Chapter 10

"Ah one, two, three. One, two, three. One, two, three," The Popps yelled over the music, tapping out the rhythm of the waltz. "Keep your heads up, backs straight. Remember ladies, your steps should be as flawless as the diamonds in your future engagement rings. *Mister* Rice, please try to leave at least a few of your partner's toes unbroken."

I winced as Bobby's feet came down hard on mine again. He smiled apologetically. It was the early days of July and the dance studio was hotter than ever. Bobby's hands positively dripped sweat and his polyester shirt was soaked through. I regretted my earlier act of kindness. Everyone else assumed they were off the hook for Bobby dance duty now that I had willingly signed up.

Between my grounding and Peggy's wedding preparations, we hadn't been alone in forever. At school, I never went for two hours without telling Peggy all my deepest, darkest secrets. Now we were being swept along two different currents and I was swimming hard to keep up with her.

"Mrs. Popple," Ella Greenwood said, timidly putting up a hand in the middle of the song. "Do you think we could get a little water? I feel a little light..."

Just like a Hollywood movie, Ella swooned right in front of us. Bobby gallantly rushed forward and caught her before she landed. Her eyelids fluttered as we crowded around.

"Back up, back up," Mrs. Popple said. "Give her some air. Mr. Rice, please take Miss Greenwood outside and bring her some water. Anyone else feeling faint?"

She cast her eyes around the room, waiting for someone to challenge her. No one dared.

"You're wasting bars. Pair up! Ah one, two, three. One, two, three," she said, observing us. "I'm going to check up on Miss Greenwood. Miss Bell, I'm sure I can trust you to put on the next song?"

Nancy nodded. As soon as The Popps left the room, we all abandoned our partners and our perfect postures, slouching off the dance floor. Nancy immediately started bragging about her new date for the ball. Every week there was another man she decided to bestow favor on. This week, it was the quarterback from our rival high school.

"All the girls from St. Bernie are so angry at me!" She said, giggling. "One of them even tried to fight me at the drive-in. And then I told Frankie to sort it out or I was going to split. I don't know where that girl gets off. Everyone knows St. Bernadette is where all the scholarship girls go to school. They're nowhere in my league."

"Hey!" said Lisa Chaplin, a St. Bernadette girl who was most definitely not on scholarship.

"Well, I didn't mean you, obviously Lisa. You're here, aren't you?" Nancy said.

That was the closest anyone had ever come to saying what was a given but never discussed. To go to the Cotillion Ball, your family needed to be a part of the club and pay the exorbitant fees. The deb lessons were an extra cost. Everyone in this room was wealthy, those outside were not.

I was lucky I was inside the room. I had my parents to thank for my privilege. So why was I so eager to throw it off?

Peggy rolled her eyes and walked over to me.

"I wish The Popps were here to tell Nancy she's not behaving with class right now," she said.

"Why don't you? She's your friend," I replied.

I still could not understand for the life of me why Peggy insisted on being friendly with Nancy. But beneath her mischievousness, Peggy was a loyal soul and she'd been friends with Nancy since kindergarten.

Peggy laughed. "Oh. Bliss. You say that like it's some kind of disfigurement. Nancy really isn't that bad. I wish you'd try to get to know her better."

"Thankfully, I won't have to," I said.

"What does that mean?" Peggy asked, her eyebrows lifted in anticipation of some hot gossip.

Finally, while Nancy and Lisa distracted the rest of the class, I told Peggy all about the scholarship to Arizona. I needed to give them an answer soon and I wanted to say yes. How could I not? It was the chance of a lifetime.

"Wow," Peggy said flatly when I finished. Her face showed none of the excitement I felt.

"Are you going to come home for my wedding?" Peggy asked. "I don't think the maid of honor can just run off to play ball."

That's all she had to say? Peggy's wedding was only one day. I was talking about the rest of my life.

"Of course I'll be there for your wedding!" I said. "How could you think I'd miss it?"

Sensing my hurt, Peggy hugged me.

"Ok then. I'm very happy for you. Congratulations, it's what you want isn't it?"

"More than anything," I said. Spoken out loud, I knew those words were the truest I'd ever said.

Peggy gestured around the room at our friends and classmates with a sad smile on her lips.

"If I were you, I'm not sure I could leave all this," she said.

We did live a charmed life, even sweaty Bobby Rice. Our futures stretched out before us like a sunny garden path. From the Cotillion Ball, we would go on to good colleges, rush the best sororities, have our engagement notices written up in the local paper, hold dream weddings, raise darling children, join the right clubs, keep nice homes, buy lakefront property, go on expensive vacations, and start the cycle again with our own children. Life was a checklist we would go down, dutifully marking each milestone off. The only stipulation was that you had to follow the rules. And I was good at rules. We'd cluck to each other when someone stepped out of bounds. What a shame she's divorced, we'd say. Remember how beautifully she danced at her debut?

Was I ready to step off that path to find happiness elsewhere? It was scary out there. There were bramble and quicksand I'd have to navigate alone.

We heard Mrs. Popple's heavy footsteps in the hallway and scrambled back into position. Bobby hadn't come back, so I paired up with Ella's partner. Nancy put the music back on, and we innocently stepped as if we'd been dancing the entire time.

"Look who I found in the hallway," Mrs. Popple said when she re-entered the studio.

She was with Michael, one hand steadying herself on his arm as if she were frail. My ass she needed help walking. Even The Popps wasn't immune to Michael's charm. All around me, girls fixed hair, wiped brows and smoothed skirts. I caught Nancy Bell unbuttoning an extra button on her silk dress and adjusting her cleavage.

"What?" She mouthed when she caught me glaring. Clearly Nancy would be willing to step in for me at any point should Michael get lonely.

Michael took in her golden tanned skin and I tasted bitter jealousy. I didn't want to leave him here unattended, ready to fall into Nancy's clutches.

"Babe!" I said, rushing forward to hug him and then, as Nancy batted her eyelashes in Michael's direction, brought him in for a slow, deep kiss.

There were appreciative hoots from the class.

"Miss Bennet! That is quite enough," Mrs. Popple snapped. The Popps was not a fan of PDA.

Michael gave me a goofy grin.

"Does this mean you want to go back to the orchards?" He asked.

I blushed and shook my head, happy his attention was focused squarely on me again. It scared me how easily it could slip from my grasp. I held him tight.

"Do you want Arizona more than that?" Peggy asked, stepping behind me, her voice in my ear.

Suddenly, I wasn't so certain of what I wanted. I pretended not to hear. I didn't have the answer to that one.

Chapter 11

"U.S.A.! U.S.A.!"

I didn't know who started the chant, but we were all doing it. Standing up and stomping our feet on the cracked linoleum of the high school cafeteria's floor. Our faces were flushed with the anticipation of what we had been asked to perform: represent the United States of America in a showdown between superpowers.

Coach had finally broken down before the team meeting and spilled the beans about the top-secret tournament. It wasn't much of a secret anymore anyway. There'd been a story about it in the local paper with a picture of the Lady Scarlets. We were going to play a girls' team from the USSR in a best-of-three fight to the finish. Daddy was right. Those Soviets thought they were so superior, they could master anything they put their minds to. They even had the stones to think they could beat us at our own game.

I thought for sure I'd have to beg Mama and Daddy to let me play, but thanks to the local press, I was golden. A few people Daddy knew recognized me in the photo and word got out that Chip Bennet's daughter was going to take on the Commies. Business partners and rivals called to wish me luck. Since I was now such a goddamn hero, it would be positively un-American to not let me play.

I crossed my arms with satisfaction. For once, Mama and Daddy's obsession with appearances had broken in my favour. There was no way they could have said no to me. It was a sign that softball was my destiny. I would win this tournament, and then they would have to let me go to Arizona. I still hadn't told them about the scholarship yet. Best to win first and then float it past them with the momentum in my favour.

The cheering stopped and we started to chatter. A few parents had come along to hear Chris Phillips from Softball USA explain the tournament. Tessa fingered her tiny gold cross pendant and muttered that the Soviets were godless. Cher wanted to know what they would be wearing when they came and Nancy wondered if the boys would find them cute.

"They'll probably all wear matching outfits," Jane said, pushing up her glasses. "After all, conformity is the point. They don't reward individualism the way we do here. They stomp it out."

I wasn't so sure we valued individualism here either. Linda had enough problems in town being Mexican, and this was supposed to be the Land of the Free.

"Who cares if they're all clones?" Susie and Deb asked in unison. "We're still going to whoop them!"

Speaking of clones... How did they do that?

"My Dad says not to look them in the eyes or they'll infect you with their deranged values," Becca said.

Jane rolled her eyes. "That's not how it works. Communism isn't a contagious disease."

Becca flushed. "It is too! They're here to recruit."

"They want us to turn our backs on Jesus!" Tessa said.

"They want to take our money and give it to the poors. Ew," Nancy said.

"They're probably coming to spy," Sharon said.

There were uneasy murmurs among the group. I shifted uncomfortably. I'd seen the movies too. Reds were dangerous. They were a nation of faceless monsters, set on destroying America. Jem was disgusted. The odds were 50/50 whether he was reacting to us or the threat of communism. Why was he even here? His obligation to the team was officially over.

"The only thing those Russian girls are coming here to do is win softball games, and we're not going to let them," a melodic voice said.

We turned to the front of the classroom to see a woman wearing a red, white, and blue tracksuit with TEAM USA written on the sleeves. A ripple of surprise ran through the room. We had all assumed Chris Phillips, the championship softball player, would be a man. Instead, Chris was a woman in her early 30s with a sleek brunette bob, hazel eyes, and a small, pert nose. If she had worn a little makeup, she could be almost pretty. She was short with a solid build. I guessed the tracksuit disguised a muscular form. The set of her mouth made me think that she was a woman who didn't tolerate many weaknesses, including her own. I automatically scanned for a wedding ring. She wasn't wearing one.

"Right ladies, listen up," Chris said. "Thanks to your stellar performance, you have been selected to represent the United States of America in the Girls of Summer Summit Series. This means you'll be playing a best of three tournament stretched over a week in Cleveland, where both teams will be staying in dorms."

Jane's hand shot up. "Why us? We're state champions, but are we the best in the country?"

"Sure we are!" Karen said.

Jane persisted. "Of course we're great, but we haven't actually played the other teams to officially decide the national championship. I guess a better question is, who decided we were the best in the country?"

Jane had a good point. Why had we been chosen to represent the USA?

Chris brushed off the question with an airy stroke of her hand. "You're good enough. Far be it from me to question the Powers That Be, but your team fit roughly fit the geographical requirements for this tournament, regardless of skill. Ohio was picked as the tournament's location before anything else was decided."

"That's not exactly a vote of confidence," Nancy said.

"Not to worry, Princess. I can guarantee that with my coaching you'd beat any team in the country."

Nancy's mouth twisted. I smirked. Chris couldn't be half-bad if she pegged Nancy that quickly.

"What about the Soviets?" I asked.

Chris considered me for a moment, her quick eyes scanning me from head to toe. "That's a good question. What's your name?"

"Bliss Bennet."

"Ah, the home run hitter."

"On a good day," I replied. She'd obviously done her homework. What else did she know about us?

"We need every day to be a good day for you from here on out. These girls have been training for this tournament since they could walk. The Russians have a fanatical devotion to their baseball program. This is just Phase 1. They want to see how prepared they are before challenging the men to a baseball game. The Reds say their men's team rivals the A's."

The World Series Champs? I scoffed. No way. Could they?

"We can take them," Linda said, her chin jutting out as she spoke.

"Linda, I assume? I like your spunk," Chris said. "We're going to need a lot of that. This isn't just some fun tournament. Our national pride rests on your shoulders."

I gulped. They must be pretty confident if they thought they could take on the best first time out.

Susie and Deb's mother cut in from the back of the room. "Excuse me, that seems like a lot of pressure for teenage girls."

Chris shrugged. "I'll tell you what, the Russians aren't thinking that. They see it as their national duty. Your daughter is free to opt-out of the tournament if she doesn't think she can take it."

"Mom," the twins hissed in unison. "We're fine."

"Good," Chris said. "Because there's more. But we'll talk about that a little later." She hesitated, biting her lip but seemed to decide not to spill it right then.

The rest of the meeting was filled with mainly boring administrative details. Where we were going, how we'd get there, Team USA policies. We had three weeks to get into fighting shape, and we'd start an intensive training camp in town two days from now. That part sounded great. I did not like the sound of the photo shoot they had planned for us. But if they dressed us cute instead of frumpy, Mama would be very pleased.

While Chris spoke I imagined what her life must be like. I didn't even know it was possible for a woman to make a living from baseball. The closest I ever thought I'd get was working as a secretary in the Indians front office. That is, if Michael were fine with his wife working outside the home, which he thought was completely pointless. What did it feel like to wake up every day and live softball?

Chris ended the meeting with a tight smile.

"Rest up, Ladies. You're going to need it."

I walked out of the classroom with Nancy. Mama and Daddy hadn't come, of course, so I had to walk home.

"Wanna ride?" Nancy offered.

Taking Peggy's advice to heart, I accepted. Nancy was clearly making an effort to be nice too.

The inside of her gleaming T-Bird was scattered with work-study applications. Nancy shoved them out of sight.

"Like I need these, right?" She asked as I uncrumpled a job description for a cafeteria server at Trinity. I tried to imagine Nancy in a hairnet and uniform instead of designer clothes. It was impossible.

"What are these for?" I asked.

"Oh, just some character-building bullshit my Dad's into. I'm so not into that. I told him I'd fill a couple out, but I've just been hiding them in my car."

It was a little late for Nancy's parents to improve her character. She was spoiled beyond repair.

She aggressively chewed her gum, making loud snapping noises.

"So what did you think of that Team USA lady? Total dyke, am I right?"

Yikes. Nancy was never one to mince words.

"How do you know that?"

Nancy gave me a knowing look over her sunglasses.

"Come on. An unmarried woman of that age? Dedicated to sports? There's no way she's not a rug muncher. Bet you any amount of money she's got a nice 'roommate' whose parents also wonder why she's never met a nice man."

"Huh."

I didn't know how to reply. Was Chris a lesbian? And if so, was she gay because she spent her life playing softball? Or did she like playing softball because she was gay? Would people say those kinds of things about me if I wanted to play softball in college?

Not for the first time, I was grateful for Michael. I had my handsome boyfriend to keep me safe from ugly rumours. As long as I had him, there wouldn't be any whispers.

Chapter 12

I knew something was off the second I walked in the front door.

First of all, there was the smell. Patchouli and incense wafted through the foyer. Then there was the strange music coming from the record player. Instead of Sinatra or Bennet, it was blasting something with twanging strings and an Oriental sound. Definitely not Mama or Daddy's choice.

I was tired from a hard day's practice. Chris had decided that our fitness levels needed improvement, and we'd spent most of the day running up and down hills. All I wanted was a long hot bath and to sleep for 12 hours before doing it all again tomorrow.

There was clanging in the kitchen and I tensed. Mama and Daddy didn't use the kitchen and Rosa was never that noisy.

"Hello?" I said and crept forward tentatively.

A baby cried. What the hell? Who was in the house?

"Hello?" I tried again, this time coming closer. A homicidal murderer wouldn't be cooking with a baby, would he? Unless he was cooking the baby.

I was ready to run out to the neighbors and call the police when Kathleen rushed out, arms and wrists jangling with bangles and bells.

"Bliss!" Kathleen said, smothering me in a long hug. The earth and patchouli smell belonged to her. I should have known. I let myself be held by my older sister. I hadn't realized just how much I'd missed her until she was here standing in front of me.

"Are Mama and Daddy home?" I asked cautiously. I meant do Mama and Daddy know you're here? The last time Kathleen had stopped by, they told her never to come back.

"Marie and Chip are otherwise engaged. I think they're staying overnight in Cleveland for some gala or another. You know, just the typical pageant of excess. Look at all your freckles!"

Kathleen held me out at arm's length and gave me an up and down. She was thinner than the last time I had seen her. Her hair, the same copper color as mine, hung down practically to her elbows. But unlike mine, it was stringy and undernourished. She wore a white kaftan with cobalt embroidery on the cuffs and what appeared to be the contents of an entire jewellery box.

There was the baby cry again.

"Kathleen, who is that?"

The smile slid from her face.

"I told you before not to call me that anymore. It's Moonbeam now. Just Moonbeam. I am a pure, shining light."

Great, this crazy stuff was still going on. I thought for sure she would have dropped this and moved onto her next phase. I much preferred Kathleen's rock goddess incarnation, when she travelled the country following the Rolling Stones and wore fur and spoke in a fake English accent. That Kathleen had a sense of humor about things. And a bit of a drinking problem. Mama,

Daddy and I had come home from the theatre a year and a half ago to find her holding court in the living room with a group of what Daddy called deviants. They' all been drinking and who knows what else and one of them had knocked over Mama's precious Ming vase.

"Out, now, all of you," Daddy had ordered.

When Kathleen protested, she tripped and fell into the glass coffee table, cutting her hand. Blood spurted out onto the white carpeting, while Mama went into a state and Kathleen's friends just laughed.

Daddy had taken off his tie and wrapped it around her hand.

"You're a goddamn mess, Kathleen. You need to leave and I don't want to see you back here until you're clean."

"Fuck you!" She had screamed and stormed off. Her friends followed after her, spilling drinks and cigarette ash on the way out.

We didn't hear anything from Kathleen for six months until she wrote to say she had met this man she called simply, "The Teacher." He encouraged her to give away her worldly goods and make peace with her family. She was accepting nature and love in her life, she wrote, and from henceforth she was to be known simply as Moonbeam. While she was pursuing the path of enlightenment, would Mama and Daddy be able to send her $1,000?

Daddy wrote the check and urged her, as he always did, to finish her college degree. We all assumed the Moonbeam phase would pass. Instead, she was still deep in it. And judging from the reddish fuzz on the top of that baby's head, the child was hers. Mama was going to freak.

"Moonbeam, who is this?"

"Why, it's Willow, of course. I wrote Mama and Daddy about their granddaughter. We're here so they can meet her."

This was the first I'd heard about Kathleen's daughter. Another topic Mama and Daddy avoided. I didn't have to ask to know that Kathleen wasn't married. The horror. Kathleen's letter must have been what sent Mama into her bedroom for three days last month.

"I can tell by your face that they didn't tell you. Unsurprisingly that they choose repression rather than live their truth. I suppose they thought this little problem would just disappear if they ignored it long enough. But we're not going anywhere!"

I cringed at the gathering storm. At least this latest disaster would take the heat off me for a while. Kathleen jiggled Willow and the baby cooed.

"Do you want to hold your niece?" She asked, and before I could answer, she thrust the swaddled bundle into my arms.

I tensed, freezing in an awkward hold. I'd never held a baby before. Willow screeched briefly before she settled.

"How old is she?" I asked.

"Four months. I think she likes you."

Willow sighed softly and nuzzled against me. I relaxed slightly. Her warm little body was soft against my chest. Her features were so tiny and perfect. I marvelled at her miniature finger-nails, the tiny veins under her closed eyelids.

Kathleen watched me.

"If you think you know love, you have no idea until you become a mother. It just splits you open and fills you with fear, and hope, and happiness."

No way I was ready for that. I could barely handle my own hope and fear.

"Who's the father?" I asked.

"It doesn't really matter," Kathleen replied. "We're here now and it's better with just the two of us. I can raise her the opposite of the way we were. With freedom from bullshit expectations."

"So Willow won't be making her debut in her eighteenth summer?" I joked.

Kathleen scoffed. "Not a chance. We don't believe in bourgeois distractions."

I sat down on the chesterfield in the living room, still holding Willow. She radiated energy and unlimited possibility. Willow wasn't beholden to the strict upbringing of our parents. She could be and do whatever she wanted.

"I can't believe I'm jealous of a baby," I said.

"Not content to subscribe to the groupthink of the wealthy? Are you sure about that? It's easier to be a sheep." Kathleen's eyes flashed with a challenge. She could be so exhausting sometimes.

Of course, it was easier to be a sheep, but I wouldn't get to do what I loved. At least Kathleen understood not living up to Mama and Daddy's expectations. I told her all about Arizona, Michael, Bryn Mawr and the Girls of Summer tournament. She didn't seem as tortured by my dilemma as I was.

"So what's the problem?" Kathleen asked. "If you want to go, just go. You aren't beholden to this place."

She made it sound so easy. But Kathleen forgot that I wasn't like her.

"I'm afraid that leaving means cutting all my ties. I want to go, but I also want to keep my place here. Is that possible?"

I wasn't as brave or headstrong as Kathleen. I couldn't just walk away from it all.

"I don't know why you give a shit," she said.

For someone who was all about peace and love, Kathleen really swore a lot.

"Because I do. My life is important to me," I said. This life was all I knew.

"You mean our parents' life. The one they had charted perfectly for you. It's all bullshit. You're nothing but another accessory in their great fraud, this grand sham of a marriage. This place is toxic, and you need to get out. Unless you like being as shallow as they are."

I sighed. Kathleen's grand pronouncements were always so dramatic.

"Then why are you back here?" I asked, pushing back.

"Mama and Daddy have more money than they know what to do with, and Willow and I need some of it. They should be happy to provide for their granddaughter."

I shook my head. Typical Kathleen. She dismissed Mama and Daddy in one breath and wanted a handout in another. She claimed to hate their lifestyle, but she liked what their money could do for her and wasn't ashamed to ask for it. I was tired of talking to her.

"I'm going to have a bath," I said, handing Willow back to Kathleen and stomping up the stairs.

I was chin-level in bubbles when Kathleen crept into the bathroom. She brushed the vanilla conditioner through my hair like when we were kids. I relaxed under her touch, pretending that we were back in easier times.

"I'm sorry, Bissy," she said, using my childhood nickname. I couldn't remember the last time anyone had called me that.

"I know that softball is important to you. Anyone can see you've been crazy about it since you were a kid. I want to help you get to Arizona. I'll get you the money you need, and I can arrange for a ride. That way, when you tell Mama and Daddy about it, they won't be able to say no. Or if they do, you won't need their permission anyway."

"Thanks, Kath- un, Moonbeam," I said.

I sunk down into the water as she gently placed the comb on the back of the toilet and walked away. I opened my eyes under the surface and watched the bubbles. A wild sensation in my chest overcame me, the heat spreading from my heart to my fingertips. The feeling was so foreign, I was afraid to name it. But it was hope, plain and simple. Hope that I had finally found the courage to make the leap to Arizona and carve out my own identity.

Chapter 13

"Okay, Bliss, this is you," Cher said from the front seat.

There were eight of us packed like clowns into her Buick after a post-practice ribbon shopping expedition. I was sprawled over four other girls in the back, draped in red, white, and blue satin.

"I'm going to need someone to open the door for me," I said, and giggled as I wormed my way off the squirming laps and collapsed onto the asphalt of my driveway. My arms, tired from endless pushups, rebelled against my weight and I landed face first. Damn it. Mama would have a conniption if I messed up my face.

"You okay?" Jane asked, getting out of the passenger seat to help me up.

"I must be delirious from practice, because that didn't hurt at all," I replied.

Jane dusted me off.

"Hey, what's Coach's car doing here?" She asked, recognizing his blue pickup.

"I'm not sure," I said, but my stomach clenched in anxiety.

"You okay? You're a little pale," Jane said.

I gave her a quick hug. "I'm fine. Just a little stress response syndrome from practice, ha ha. Don't make me go back!"

Jane was too smart to be fooled by my fake cheerful response, but smart enough to let it go.

"Alright, see you tomorrow," she said. "Good luck with whatever it is."

It was deathly quiet inside the house. I suspected Kathleen would be nowhere to be found. She knew how to dodge a downer when she saw one coming.

"Hello?" I called.

God, I was tired of coming home to weird surprises.

"We're in here," Mama said with fake cheer.

Sitting on the couches stiffer than Nixon in China, were Mama, Daddy, and Coach. Daddy's jaw jumped as he clenched and unclenched his fists. Coach was weary and Mama smiled like she was at a church picnic.

"Bliss, honey," Mama said, holding her arms out and making room for me next to her. "Wilfred was just telling us all about your scholarship to Arizona."

I willed the ground to open up and swallow me whole. Shit. This wasn't the plan.

"*Mister* Christie says that you've known for some time. When were you planning on telling us?" Daddy asked, refusing to use Coach's first name.

"Sorry, kid. I thought you would have told them by now. Arizona needs an answer ASAP," Coach said.

"You can just tell them no, Bliss has already accepted to Bryn Mawr," Daddy said.

The air went out of the room.

"But Daddy — "

Daddy held up his hand. "But nothing. It's already been decided. And I don't need some other man coming into my house and telling me what's best for my daughter."

His voice raised with every word until he practically yelled the word daughter. Mama fanned herself frantically, her eyes darting back and forth to the stairs. No doubt she wanted to make a break for her nerve pills upstairs. Coach was grim and out of place in our gilded sitting room in his dusty sweatsuit.

"Chip —" Coach said, but Daddy cut him off.

"It's Mr. Bennet to you. Just like she's MRS. Bennet," he said.

"Chip," Mama tried. "Wilfred is just here delivering some good news about Bliss."

"And with that, I think I'll be taking my leave," Coach said and heaved himself off the couch.

Oh, why did he have to come here and ruin things? I was handling this on my own. Now Mama and Daddy would be too angry to even hear me out. I didn't follow Coach to say goodbye.

We sat in silence as the front door closed behind him and his car started up.

"Bliss," Mama said. "That was so embarrassing for us. What an unpleasant scene you caused. Why didn't you tell us about this softball scholarship? You know we don't approve."

"That could be why," I said.

"Don't be smart with your mother," Daddy snapped. "You're lucky that we're letting you play in this tournament at all. You can believe that Arizona is off the table."

My face heated. "Why did you have to be so rude to Coach about it? He thought he was here delivering good news."

"Oh, is that what he was here for?" Daddy asked and Mama shot him a quick glare. What was that about? "My impression was that he was here to tear apart my family and take my daughter away. I am not going to let that happen. In fact, I don't want you to see that man ever again."

I stood up too, my hands shaking. "How is that even possible? He's the Coach of our team!"

"A team that I will no longer allow you to play for."

I panicked, scrambling for an argument. No, no, no. This couldn't be happening. Coach's visit was going to ruin everything.

"Are you joking me? It's too late! I can't back out now. The team needs me. We're a week away from the tournament! I can't just be replaced now that I've already committed. Do you know how bad that would look?"

"I don't care," Daddy said.

Mama put a hand on his arm to steady him. "Chip honey, people would ask a lot of questions if Bliss were to suddenly drop out. Why don't we let her finish up her little tournament and that will be the end of it."

"My little tournament?" I said, my voice getting shriller. Now I was the one who yelled. "My little tournament? Just the little tournament that's turned into an international affair? The one that's going to show the Soviets they can't beat us at our own way of life? THAT little tournament??"

If preserving our public reputation couldn't sway, maybe my patriotic duty would help. I was desperate to keep playing and furious that they wanted to take this away from me.

"Bliss, you show your mother some respect," Daddy said.

"Why don't you try doing the same for me?" I asked. "And another thing, I am going to Arizona."

Daddy guffawed. "How will you get there without any money?"

Even in the heat of anger, I knew better than to bring Kathleen into it.

"I've worked it out. I'll get there on my own and then the scholarship should take care of the rest. You can't stop me."

I lifted my chin in defiance. I was breathless. I'd never stood up to Mama and Daddy like this before.

Daddy's normally warm eyes blackened.

"If you go there, don't bother to come back," he said.

He stormed from the room, leaving Mama and me alone in shock. I moaned. Why, oh why had I defied Daddy like that? This isn't the way I wanted it to go. Damn that Coach. What had I just done?

Chapter 14

I tiptoed around Mama and Daddy for the next week. Mama teared up in my presence, and Daddy only spoke to me in short sharp bursts when absolutely necessary. Focusing on the tournament was the only thing that kept me going. They would forgive me when we won. In the meantime, I avoided them as much as possible, ducking out of the house in the early morning for practice and hiding in my room as soon as I got home.

It was easy to go to bed early. Chris was hell-bent on making us sharper, stronger players. We ran for miles, skipped rope for hours, and did pushups, squats, and sit ups until our muscles gave out. Jem, who usually silently observed drills from the dugout joined us for training. His dark skin glowed with sweat from the effort.

After we were exhausted from conditioning, the practice would start. Endless throwing, catching, and batting drills. Complicated games designed to sharpen our instincts. On the first day, Chris threw a ball at Becca's head while Coach gave us instructions. Unprepared, it hit Becca square on the cheek and the hollow sound of smacked flesh echoed in the field. We gasped in shock. She cried but Chris didn't apologize.

"Why didn't you catch that?" She asked as Becca sobbed louder. "Do you think you'll get a warning during a game when a ball's coming at you? Be prepared."

We were wary. What kind of psycho were we dealing with here?

Later that day, she chucked a ball at Linda's temple during a water break. Linda's hand flew up lightning quick and gripped the ball.

"Better," Chris said.

We wore our gloves at all times, eyeing Chris's movements with suspicion.

Our bodies paid the price of her workouts. I came home battered and exhausted. It took all my strength to lower myself into the bathtub at the end of the day. If Michael wanted to take me out, he had to practically carry me into the car. Finally, I just begged off our dates until the tournament was over. I didn't have the energy for them, and I didn't have the strength to resist his advances either. I still hadn't told him about Arizona and when he chatted away about Fall, I didn't correct him. I was waiting until my plans were set.

The worst were the days when I also had Deb class after practice. The Popps caught me asleep during etiquette and called Mama to complain about my lack of courtesy and unkempt appearance.

Surprisingly, Kathleen and Willow's visit didn't go nuclear. After the shock wore off, Mama and Daddy were pleased with their tiny granddaughter. Mama left the house twice before noon with Kathleen to shop for Willow. Daddy called her his little munchkin, stopping often to nuzzle her peach fuzz head.

Of course, peace never lasted long with Kathleen. I came home one day to a shouting match between Kathleen and Mama and Daddy. Mama had taken Kathleen and Willow to the salon, where they had run into friends from the club. While they cooed over Willow, Mama implied that Kathleen was a Vietnam widow. One of them said it was a shame Willow would grow up without a father because of those godless savages.

Kathleen told the woman that Willow's father was alive and well and he would never, under any circumstances be her husband. She stormed out of the salon, foils still in her hair. Mama had to apologize to all the ladies she knew and gather up Willow alone. When I got home, Kathleen was screaming at Mama for being such a dedicated phony.

"Why are you so obsessed with what everyone thinks?" She shrieked.

"Why don't you care an ounce about social convention?" Mama countered.

"Because the whole system is messed up. Why should I participate in your farce just so I don't accidentally make anyone uncomfortable?"

I lurked on the edge of the room. Kathleen did have a point. Why was it her job to make everyone else feel ok about their choices?

"You'll participate if you want that handout you came here to get," Daddy said.

"This is why I want to check out. What kind of society doesn't provide for its youngest? Mothers should be celebrated and supported. The Soviets at least get that right," Kathleen said.

I cringed. There was no way Kathleen would when an argument with Daddy by complementing the Commies.

"The only thing the Soviets are interested in is breeding more monsters. If Willow were born in the USSR, she'd be taken away from you in a split second if she showed any aptitude for anything, and you'd be back in the mill or the factory, instead of holed up in your parents' cushy home," Daddy said.

"You know what, you're nothing but a pig," Kathleen said.

"Kathleen!" Mama said.

"It's Moonbeam," she replied. "Now say goodbye to your granddaughter. I won't let you infect her with your toxic ideologies."

I sighed. Kathleen's dramatic exit would be more upsetting if she hadn't done it a million times already.

Mama cradled Willow while Kathleen banged around upstairs, packing her things. After a prolonged silence, Daddy followed her up.

"I hope you put your jewelry in the safe, Marie," he said.

He returned minutes later, gripping Kathleen by the elbow. She thrashed under his iron grip. Mama started to cry. Willow wailed.

"Let me go, you fascist!" Kathleen screamed.

"Give your sister back her brooch," he said.

"Why don't you just buy her a new one?"

"Because that one belongs to her and I'm not having you pawn it off to buy dope. Now give it," he said. His voice was steel.

With a shaking hand, Kathleen held out my diamond circle pin.

"Oh, Kathleen," Mama sobbed.

"Bliss, come and take your brooch," Daddy said.

Without meeting Kathleen's eyes, I crept forward and took it, ashamed. I was such an idiot. Why hadn't I thought of selling my jewelry for airfare to Arizona? But I didn't really think of them as mine to sell. Most of my pieces had been passed down. The brooch had belonged to Grandmother. Mama said I didn't really own these things, I was just holding them for the next generation. Without a doubt, Kathleen's heirlooms were long gone.

For a fleeting moment, I considered letting Kathleen keep it. Daddy's stormy face made me lose my nerve. Oh, Kathleen must hate me. I was such a goddamn coward. She'd never help me get to Arizona now.

"Kathleen," Daddy said. "I think your visit is over."

She shook him off but didn't correct him on her name.

"Let me say goodbye to my sister at least," she said.

Before I could say anything, she held me in a tight hug.

"Don't worry, Bliss. I'll come to find you before your bus leaves tomorrow," she whispered in my ear. "We have to get you out of here."

Dangerous hope flickered in my chest.

"That's enough," Daddy said.

Kathleen took the wailing Willow from Mama's arms, grabbed her suitcase and stood at the door.

'Well," she said.

Daddy sighed and took his wallet from the back pocket. He removed all his cash and without counting, handed the wad to Kathleen.

"Don't come back here anymore," he said. "It upsets your mother."

Kathleen slammed the door on her way out and the silence that followed was as deafening as Willow's screams. Hurt was etched all over their faces. Would they look like that when I took off across the country? Without saying a word, Mama, Daddy, and I all went our separate ways.

Chapter 15

The team ride crunched into the high school parking lot, sending gravel flying. It was an extra large school bus, re-purposed of our use, painted eggshell white with TEAM USA screaming on the side in red and white bubble letters and surrounded by an explosion of yellow stars. Everyone would see us coming. Chris said that was the point. Jane dubbed the bus Big Bertha.

"Dibs on the back!" Susie and Deb said, skipping aboard.

"Not so fast," Nancy said. "I called a backbench."

I let them rush by. I was busy searching past them, straining my eyes for Kathleen. She said she would meet me with a name and some money. There was no sign of her yet, but it was Kathleen's way to do things at the absolute last minute. She'd swan in any second on a puff of dope smoke.

I leaned back on Bertha, waiting. Linda slid in beside me. She seemed to be the only one who wasn't jangling with nerves. Her dark, wavy hair was pulled back into a no-nonsense ponytail.

"When those *pendejas* are done fighting for seats without air circulation, I'll go in and grab an airy seat up front. You with me?" She asked.

"I'm waiting for someone," I replied.

"Ah yes, that handsome man of yours."

I didn't correct her. Michael had already dropped me off and left. He had things to do today and it was pointless for him to wait around.

"Are you going to miss him when you go away?" Linda asked.

I'd been so worried about Michael waiting for me, I'd never considered if I'd miss him. I squinted in Linda's direction. No sign of Kathleen.

"I'm not sure I'm going to go to Arizona," I said. The words tasted bitter in my mouth.

"Did you get into another program too?" Linda asked with excited curiosity.

"No, I meant, I'm not sure if I'm going to play softball next year," I said.

"Huh?" Linda said like she was talking to one of those crazies outside of the liquor store. "Maybe you're the *pendeja*. You're not going to college?"

"No, it's not like that. My parents want me to go to Bryn Mawr. It's all been arranged."

"Ah, I see. Crema problems," she said, rolling her big brown eyes. "If I don't play, I don't go to college. I'm going to be the first one in my family. My moms can hardly believe it. But I told her, where's your faith now? Of course, I got a scholarship. She lights enough candles to burn down the church and sprinkles holy water on me while I sleep. She's been currying a lot of favor with the Big Man to help my pitching. I don't have the heart to tell her I'm good because I practice. She makes me go to confession once a week. Every Saturday I go in there and apologize for loving baseball more than I love my mother. I love Moms, but I really love playing, you know what I mean?"

Linda tightened her ponytail. Her face was baby fat round, obscuring her bone structures. You could tell that one day she would be truly beautiful. Especially if she smiled, which she rarely did. Linda was the most focused member on our team, rarely joking around between innings. This was the most she had ever revealed about herself. She was both proud and ashamed of her confession. Mostly Linda hoped I understood her. I did. More than anything.

"Yeah. I'm with you," I said.

Linda broke into one of her rare grins and punched me lightly on the arm.

"I thought you might be, chica. Anyway, I told Moms she needs to save some prayers for Manny. That kid is out of control."

I met Linda's little brother once. He was cute, if cocky. I heard he got arrested last year. Kind of like Kathleen.

"I know what that's like," I said.

Linda gave me a knowing look. Everyone has a Kathleen story.

"All aboard, ladies!" Coach yelled from inside the bus.

Linda straightened, readjusted her bag.

"Listen, I was wondering if you wanted to room with me in Cleveland. I've seen how hard you've been working. I want a roomie who isn't here just to have fun. You know Karen's my girl, but she's always dealing with all the other girls' silly problems. I don't want to hear any boy trouble tears in the middle of the night."

"Sure," I said. "Thanks for asking." I hoped some of Linda's steely nerves would rub off on me.

"You coming?" She asked, climbing the steps.

I shook my head. "I'm still waiting for someone."

I checked my watch again. Where the hell was Kathleen? She said she would be here. I could hear Chris doing roll call inside, but I stubbornly stayed outside the bus. Kathleen would come.

Finally, a woman with long hair approached in the distance. My heart lept to my throat. I shouldn't have doubted Kathleen. She was going to come through for me and show me the way to Arizona. But it wasn't her. My throat closed up.

Jem popped his head out the bus while I was on the verge of tears. I scowled and crossed my arms. His attitude was the last thing I wanted to deal with right now.

"Coach sent me to come to get you," he said. "Everything okay?"

The sympathy in his voice undid me. The tears spilled for real.

"Hey, don't cry now," he said, clearly uncomfortable. He patted my arm gruffly. His kindness only made me sob harder.

"She said she would come," I said.

"Who?" He asked. "Bliss, tell me what's wrong."

Jem never used my first name. I really was a mess. He put two large hands on my shoulders and held me at arm's length, searching my eyes with his. There was an unexpected ring of gold around his pupils.

"Kathleen. She's supposed to help me get to Arizona for school. She's going to bring me money and figure out a ride. I told her I would meet her here, but she hasn't come yet. My parents don't want me to go. She's my last hope," I said with a sob.

I cringed, waiting for his scorn. I was a foolish, spoiled girl who didn't even have enough money to her name to buy a bus ticket to Arizona. I should have gotten a job at the mall like everyone else. But when would I have time to work between baseball and deb practice? And why would I ever work a minimum wage job when Mama or Daddy just gave me money whenever I needed it?

Instead, Jem nodded. He understood.

"Okay. I'll put coach off for a little bit. I can probably buy you 10 minutes at most."

He climbed back on the bus.

"What's wrong with Bennet? She coming?" Coach asked.

Jem slid back into his usual sullen personality.

"Yeah, yeah. She says she's got woman problems or something. She needs some air. I didn't ask too much more, because frankly, I don't care."

"Thank you for contributing your excellent investigative skills," Coach replied, sarcastic.

I rolled my eyes at Jem's explanation and tried not to be too embarrassed that he mentioned my time of the month. I didn't want him knowing that I did any of that stuff.

The minutes crawled while I waited for Kathleen, anxiety creeping up my spine. I expected Coach to make me leave at any moment. Finally, I had to accept that she wasn't coming. The spark of hope I had let flame in my chest went out, leaving behind a smoking empty hole.

Chris came out to get me.

"We can't wait any longer," she said. She had changed into a new tracksuit for the occasion. This one was white with red and blue stars. She wore a matching sweatband around her head. "I have some Midol in my bag if you need any."

"I'll be fine," I said.

She could have cut off my foot and I wouldn't have felt anything. I was numb.

Slowly, I climbed the steps behind her onto the bus. I had better enjoy this tournament. It was going to be my last.

Chapter 16

Big Bertha parked outside Cleveland State University's first-year dorms, a bland, industrial building. We'd be staying there for the duration of the tournament, us on one floor, Soviets on another, and shared mealtimes in the cafeteria. A small group of reporters and photographers had gathered to wait for our arrival.

I gulped. This was for real. I wished desperately Peggy could be here with me.

"Listen up," Chris said from the front of the bus, clutching her clipboard. "I don't want anyone on this team talking to any members of the press. You got that? I want you 100% focussed on this tournament. Any media requests go through me. Someone wants to talk to you? Take your picture? Send them my way."

"Aren't we going to get to do any interviews?" Nancy asked, pouting.

Chris narrowed her eyes. "First of all, you're here to play ball, not become media darlings. But yes, you can expect some interviews, which I will arrange. I assume I should put you down in the interested column for talking to the media?"

Nancy reapplied her sheer lip gloss.

"Most definitely," she said, not catching any of the sarcasm in Chris's voice.

Jane caught my eye across the aisle and rolled hers in Nancy's direction.

"She's going to make us seem like airheads," she hissed.

Linda overheard Jane and shrugged. "I don't care what people think, as long as we come back winners."

I nodded in agreement. If Nancy wanted to parade in front of cameras, that was fine. It would give me more time to study tape and work out my swing.

"Ready, ladies?" Coach barked.

We followed behind him as camera lenses flared.

Immediately, Chris sheltered us from the press. "Hold off, please. We'll do a posed team photo and that's it."

Resigned, the photographers stopped snapping until Chris arranged us against the bus.

"Are we supposed to smile or be serious?" Becca asked.

"Give us a smile, love," a reporter said. He was short and balding, with an English accent.

"How does it feel to be playing in this tournament?" He asked.

Chris answered.

"The girls feel good. They're ready to play for their country and they're ready to win."

"Do you feel nervous?"

Some of us nodded yes.

"Any nerves will disappear as soon they step out on the field," Chris said. The way she could instantly come up with the right thing to say was amazing. "And if you'll excuse us, we need to drop our things off and head to the dining hall."

But the English reporter wasn't finished. "How are you coping with the pressure of the diplomatic wager?"

What was this guy talking about?

"As I said, they're fine," Chris said brusquely. "Now we really need to be going."

"What in the world did that guy mean?" Jane asked as we followed Chris to the dorms.

"I have no clue," I replied. A diplomatic wager sounded like a big deal. I tried not to think about it. I didn't need anything else making me nervous.

Chris escorted us upstairs to our rooms. Linda and I got a cramped pink room with bunk beds. Sunlight streamed faintly through the grimy window, illuminating the dust that spun through the air. Crochet blankets covered thin sheets bleached out from endless washings.

"Isn't this great?" Linda said. "I call bottom bunk!" She flung herself onto the mattress with glee.

"So this is what a dorm room is like," I said, putting my bag down. The space was about a quarter of the size of my bedroom at home.

"A sneak peek at college life," Linda said, smiling.

I struggled to return her smile. I'd live somewhere like this in Arizona. And I'd have to share it. Linda might be excited by the prospect, but it was a reality check for me. This was how you lived when you went to a state school, in a room with a dirty mattress and a tired paint job. Mama would have a fit.

Karen poked her head into our room. Her long blond hair had been braided into an elaborate updo. Normally she was not one to fuss with grooming and our curious looks registered.

"Cher's handiwork," she said, patting her head. "I'm here to collect you for dinner. We have to be there at six for speeches and whatnot. I think we should go down as a team."

The other girls were clumped in the hallway. Chris was passing out new jerseys.

"Put these on over your clothes," she said. "I want to show them that we're a unit. They aren't only ones who know how to put forward a collective front."

I imagined rows and rows of Russian automatons, trained from birth to defeat American girls at softball. Daddy said that children with athletic potential were taken from their parents from a young age and trained to bring glory to their country. Had the Soviets really been preparing for this that long? My palms started to sweat a little. I was committed, but was I on their level? Were any of us? We only had to drive a couple of hours down the road to get to this tournament. They came from the other side of the world. And they didn't come this far to lose.

I took my new shirt from Chris. It was a pristine white v-neck, with the short sleeves and collar ringed in red, white, and blue. Team USA was written in the same bubble letters as on Big Bertha and starbursts flared around the lettering. My number and last name were written in cherry red on the back. Spotting the number three, I instinctively drew it three times on the floor with my toe.

Jane watched me.

"Maybe we should check you for compulsive disorder," she said.

"What's that?" I asked. Jane was going to Columbia for pre-med in the fall. It wasn't unusual for her to toss out some medical terms I didn't understand. "This is just something I do to help us win."

She widened her eyes at me. "Sure, Bliss. Let me know if voices start telling you to do things, okay?"

"Shut up," I said, laughing. I wasn't the only one who had stupid things she had to do to keep our streak going. You never messed with the streak.

Our group shuffled after Chris, uncharacteristically quiet. Just outside the doors, we paused.

"What are you girls scared of?" Coach asked. "It's just a bunch of damn Commies. Let's go!"

He kicked open the double doors and we streamed behind him, chins raised a little higher.

The serving hall had been arranged so it was empty except for two long tables, one for each team. A giant framed portrait of President Nixon hung on the wall, overlooking the scene. Hot food stations ran along one side of the room, with drinks and cold items on the other side. I couldn't figure out if the fishy smell was what was for dinner, or just leftover stink from an unpleasant past meal. With the scuffed linoleum floors and paprika curtains, it reminded me of my old summer camp mess hall.

The chatter at the Russian table stopped as we eyed each other. They were the same age and had the same hairstyles. They wore their red and yellow jerseys. If the writing on their shirts weren't weird symbols, they could have been any girls from Ohio.

"They look just like us!" Becca said.

"Of course they do," Jane, the ever-practical said. "What were you expecting?"

Monsters. Little red-eyed vixens here to destroy us. They went back to talking and laughing with each other. We didn't speak the same language, but I had a hunch they were covering the same three things we always talked about: school, boys, and baseball. I started to relax.

We took our seats at the long table set up for us. We'd eat every meal at a set time in this cafeteria, Chris explained. Missing a meal was unacceptable. Every team member needed to be accounted for at all times. The rules were more for the Soviet girls than us, she explained. They were on a very tight leash.

"Right, now sit tight. I believe the mayor is going to say a few words," Chris said.

A fat, red-faced man in his 60s wheezed to the front of the room and gave a welcome speech as cameras flashed in his face. The pushy English reporter jumped in at the end.

"What about this wager that's happening?"

"We have no fear of losing Northern Lights. We are confident she will remain in Ohio long after this tournament is over."

Who the hell was Northern Lights?

"They bet a horse on us?!" Jane said, shocked.

"Not just any horse, a Triple Crown winner," Chris corrected her. "Brezhnev likes horses."

Suddenly, it clicked. Like Daddy, Mayor Reed Harper was a steel man. But his other passion was racehorses. He owned a whole stable of them. The most famous being Northern Lights. Mama loved that horse and followed it all the way through its Triple Crown victory.

"Maybe it's time you gave the girls the rest of the story," Coach said.

Chris narrowed her eyes. "I was hoping we'd never have to get into this sideshow."

Mayor Harper was so proud of his Buckeye girls competing in this tournament, he'd been blustering to every news outlet that would listen that he'd bet his most prized possession on a Team USA victory, Chris explained. And one day, the Chairman of the Soviet Union called his bluff. If Team USA lost, he wanted Northern Lights. I gulped. Holy hell, if that horse wound up in Siberia, Mama would stay in bed for weeks.

"What does Harper get if we win?" Jane asked.

"A Faberge egg," Chris replied.

Jane made a not-bad face. "Nice, let's win an egg for Cleveland."

Becca was confused. "Who bets a horse for an egg? That seems unfair to me."

Nancy rolled her eyes. "It's not a real egg, spaz. It's like, priceless jewelry."

"And it's really none of our concern. I do not want you to spend a millisecond of time thinking about any of this. Now go eat," Chris snapped, ending the conversation.

We took our trays up to the serving banquets. Meatloaf and mashed potatoes. Normal food, thank God.

"Don't be shy with the taters," I said. My deb dress be damned, I needed to fuel up.

As the server ladled a second scoop on my tray, a shadow hovered over my left shoulder. I turned around. A slight brunette with a foxy face and sharp bright blue eyes stood in front of me. Her pointy chin jutted out as she took me in.

"Can I help you?" I asked.

This wasn't the first time a competitor had tried to rattle me before a game. The secret was to keep my head high and never break eye contact. I didn't want to show weakness and let her think she'd shaken me.

"You are Bliss Bennet," the girl said. She spoke English with a heavy Russian accent. The words came out thick and husky.

"Yeah, so?"

"I read about you in paper. You are the American princess."

I flushed slightly. Goddamn the Elmhurst rag for running a picture of me from prom.

"I'm not sure what kind of info you get from Pravda, but we don't have royalty in America," I replied, trying to show her she couldn't rattle me.

"No, but you are rich like princess. You are the big hitter, yes?"

I shrugged noncommittally.

"I am Valentina Lysenko. I am pitcher. I swear that I will strike you out. You should save time and go home now."

I laughed, but it came out hollow. There was something about the intensity of this girl that was scary. I had no doubt she would do everything in her power to deliver on that promise. I struggled to stay cool.

"We'll see about that," I said.

We stared each other down until we were distracted by a symphony of giggles at the cold food table.

Jem was in the middle of a group of Russian girls attempting to unsuccessfully open a jar of pickles. In one fluid motion, Valentina strode over to him, plucked the jar from his hands, banged it off the table, and opened it with ease. She handed the jar back to Jem with a seductive smile.

"I am Valentina. If you need anything else," she said and sashayed back to her table.

I scowled at her retreating back and carried my tray back to the team table. Coach was in the middle of a lecture about fraternization.

"You will see these girls during official events. You will see them on the field. You will see them in the dining hall. But you do not need to be talking to them more than necessary, you hear? The last thing I need is a goddamn international incident on my hands, so you just keep among yourselves. That goes for all team personnel," he said, with a pointed nod at Jem.

Jem's ears stuck out a little too much. In kind of a cute way. I noticed this because they colored under Coach's scrutiny.

I clenched my jaw. What was Jem so embarrassed about? Why was Coach warning him about not getting friendly with the Russian girls? Did he have a thing for that little Slavic hussy? Was she trying to mess with me by flirting with Jem? Well, she was barking up the wrong tree. I had a boyfriend back home who was a way better catch than our assistant coach.

Jane elbowed me in the side.

"What did that chick say to you? You're wound up," she said.

I lifted my hands off my lap. I'd left tiny angry red crescent moons from digging my nails into my thighs.

"Nothing I can't deal with," I said.

Who cared who Jem thought was pretty anyway?

Chapter 17

I slept fitfully on our first night in the narrow dormitory bed. We had one more day of practice before the first game, and the nerves were starting to eat at me. All of my dreams were pinned to how this tournament panned out and it wasn't going to be the cakewalk I'd hoped it would be.

Kathleen's promise to get me to Arizona had been the closest I'd come to a realistic plan, but I had to face the truth: I couldn't do this on my own. There was no way I could just up and move clear across the country without Mama and Daddy's help. I didn't know anything about anything. What if I needed to go to the doctor? Did I need to buy my own sheets for my bed? How was I supposed to pay for those?

I punched my pillow and rolled over. I had to be good, I had to be good, I had to be good. If I could hit a game-winning home run and win a jewelled egg and wind up on the cover of USA Today as a hero and *then* tell everyone that I was going to Arizona State, Mama and Daddy would be forced to play along. Hell, they'd be so proud of me, they'd be thrilled to let me go wherever I wanted. It would be good for Daddy's business to have an American hero for a daughter. He could put me in advertisements, give people another reason to buy American instead of that cheap foreign crap that was flooding the market.

"Americans do the job right," the ad could say. Or something like that. I'd be wearing my uniform and holding a trophy or a medal or whatever we got for winning and just beaming. I'd have my hair down though. And I'd wear my signature red lipstick, even if Mama thought it clashed with my hair and I should stick to light coral colors.

At some point, while imagining my triumphant steel ad campaign, I fell asleep. Linda shook me awake for breakfast. My mouth was desert dry. The mood in the dining hall was even more raucous than last night. Jem cringed at the giggles and shrieks that surrounded him. Not in the mood to talk, I sat down next to him. We ate our oatmeal in silence.

"I can't believe we're forced to stay in this dump," Nancy said across the table. "It's positively third world, right Bliss? I mean those beds. Ughh. I'm surprised I didn't throw my back out, the mattress was so thin and saggy. I'm tempted to ask Coach if I can just book into a hotel. I don't think I can take a week of this."

I blushed a little, embarrassed to hear my thoughts echoed in Nancy's rude rant. It sounded so much worse coming from her mouth. Linda thought our room was pretty great, but at home, she shared a room with her two sisters.

"Suck it up, princess," Jem said, surprising us. "Do you know how lucky you are to have this opportunity? Think of those Russian girls. This is probably luxurious to them."

Shamed, I said nothing. I hope Jem didn't think I was as stuck up as Nancy.

"Practice in 60 minutes," Coach announced. "We'll be at the diamond just east of here. Or, for those who are directionally challenged, go out the front door and take the path to the right. DO NOT turn left. You'll end up in Siberia. Haha." He chuckled at his own joke.

I slipped out to change into my gear, walking quickly. Impatient for the elevator, I took the stairs, running two at a time. I was filled with nervous energy and burst onto our floor. Something was off. Unnerved, I realized my mistake. I was in the wrong place. This floor was near-identical, but with slight changes, like those old pictures games where you had to spot the differences.

The carpeting had a different pattern and the hallway paint was a slightly different shade of grey. A different dusty plant sat next to the elevator. I'd accidentally wound up on the Soviets' floor and I needed to get out of there ASAP. Loud sobs came from down the hall.

Whoever that was was in serious pain. The tears were heavy and gasping. I crept toward the room where the sound came from. The door was ajar and sunlight streamed into the hallway.

"Hello?" I called, poking my head in.

Facedown on the bed was a long-limbed girl with cascading blond curls.

"Are you okay?" I asked.

She started and turned her head toward me. She had big brown eyes in a heart-shaped face. Except for all the cry-induced swelling, she was beautiful.

"What are you doing here?" She asked. Like Valentina, she spoke English with a heavy accent.

They knew us so much better than we knew them. You wouldn't catch anyone on our team speaking that much Russian.

"I'm sorry," I said. "I just accidentally came up to the wrong floor and then I heard crying. I thought I would see what was wrong. Are you okay? Want me to get someone for you?"

My words caused a fresh wave of tears and I cringed.

"No one can help me," the girl said. "My heart is cracked."

She threw herself back on the bed, wailing. I perched at the end of her bed. Excessive crying made me deeply uncomfortable. Everyone in my family, really. That's why Mama just shut herself in her bedroom and the rest of us acted like nothing was wrong.

"At least it's not broken," I said, laughing weakly.

My pun didn't land. Clearly she hadn't mastered our idioms yet.

"Are you making fun of me?" She asked.

"No, it was a stupid joke," I said with regret. She seemed to be in real pain. Funny, automatons weren't supposed to cry. They told us the Russians were deeply unsentimental. This girl was far from detached.

"So who's the guy?" I asked.

"Sasha!" She said, turning his name into a howl. "See this! He mailed this letter here for me so I would get it when he arrived!"

She waved a letter in my face. The writing was hieroglyphics to me. I couldn't make out what she wanted me to see.

"I'm sorry. I can't read that," I said.

The girl huffed and snatched back the letter.

"It says, *Dear Katarina* — so formal! He only ever called me Kata — *I did not want to distract you while you were training for this important tournament* — oh, but he thinks this is good, to ruin me before I play? — *but I have felt for some time that we have grown apart. It is better if we end our relationship now before anyone gets hurt* — too late! too late! I know that he has left me for that silly Svetlana! Maybe if I wore dresses cut low every day and curled my hair instead of contributing to our country, he would pick me!"

She broke into a fresh batch of sobs. I watched her for a while. Jesus. Is this love? There's no way I'd break down like that if Michael ended it with me. I'd keep my dignity, at least.

"Sounds like Sasha's a real asshole," I said.

"A what?" Kata asked.

"Um, like a jerk. You know, a bad guy."

"Assss-hole," Kata said, stretching the word out. The crying stopped. "You mean, like a.." She pointed to her butt.

I nodded. Kata smiled, showing her crooked teeth.

"Just don't say that one around any of the adults okay? And don't mention you learned it from me," I added, remembering coach's fraternization warning. "Do you feel better? I should probably get out of here. I'm not allowed to be on this floor."

"Yes, I am better. Thank you for showing me that Sasha is the asshole," she said. "What is your name?"

"Bliss," I said. "Bliss Bennet."

Kata smiled again. "Like true happiness?"

"Something like that," I said, feeling very far from true happiness.

"Thank you, Bliss. I will see you on the field. I'm sorry you have to lose," she said. Even in distress, she was on message.

I smiled. "Yeah, yeah. We'll see about that one."

I quickly left the room, sneaking down the hallway and into the stairwell. I didn't know what to make of Kata, crying alone in her room over a boy. She seemed so... normal. Nothing like the monsters we were told to expect. I scampered up the stairs and my nerves started to fade. I had no clue how to fight monsters. But real girls? I could beat those.

Chapter 18

My sides ached as we walked off the field. A strong center was the key to a strong bat, Chris insisted, so we'd spent an hour sitting in an upright V, twisting medicine balls from side to side.

I heard the squealing before I saw him.

"Bli-iss," Becca cooed. "Michael is here."

He stood leaning on the side of the equipment shed, his collared shirt open just enough to show off his smooth chest and his Saint Eligius medallion. Michael and his family weren't Catholic — Mama would never approve if they were — but a necklace of the patron saint of metalworkers was a tradition in his steel-owning family. It was a little dumb. I mean, no one in his family actually lifted a finger to work with the metal. But like so many other opinions, I kept that to myself.

Nancy had beat me to Michael and was leaning beside him, giggling at his words. She had looped the bottom of her practice uniform through the collar of her shirt, creating a low-cut crop top. I rolled my eyes. It wasn't that damn hot out.

"Hel-llo," I said as I approached, drawing out the word and arching my brow at Nancy. "Shouldn't you be hitting the showers?" I asked her.

She took the cue to scram and skipped off with one last inviting glance at Michael over her shoulder. Nancy was too much.

"Hey babes," he said, leaning in for a kiss. He tasted like spearmint and cigarettes.

"Have you been smoking?" I asked. So disgusting.

He shrugged. "Maybe a couple. But the gum covers up the taste. Listen, I'd like to take you out for a steak dinner tonight. You think the lesbo will let you?"

I flinched at the sneering way he referred to Chris.

"I don't know if she's actually a lesbian," I hissed, making sure no one had overheard. Chris was busy supervising the cleanup of equipment. She wasn't the right person to ask if I could go out with my boyfriend for the night.

"Let me ask Coach," I said.

We were in business as long as I was back for curfew.

"Now you need to hit the showers," Michael said. "Don't be afraid to put on something a little sexy."

That was Nancy's department. But an hour later, I was wearing my most cleavage-baring dress in the squeaky leather booth of a smoky Cleveland steakhouse.

I was just getting to the menu when Michael ordered me a glass of wine, informed the server how I liked my meat cooked, and started talking about his father's steel company.

"The problem is, we're trying to compete with the cheap imports. They have a size advantage over us. All of these family-run businesses aren't going to be able to keep up in a matter of time," he said.

I half-listened as Michael rambled about the price of iron ore, labor issues, and the steel executive, and let my mind wander to something Chris said about my batting today. I needed to torque more with my back leg to generate greater power.

Guilty, I nodded and hummed at the right places but wouldn't have been able to repeat anything to save my life. Michael's eyes were bright and his cheeks flushed. He took great gulps from his wine glass. The steel industry was his real passion. I couldn't tell you stainless from alloy.

"So," I said, swirling my glass. I didn't like the sour taste of wine. "Chris thinks that if I can work on the mechanics of my swing, I'm guaranteed at least one home run a game."

"That's great, but don't you just have the three games left? When are you going to use that?" Michael asked.

I flushed. Now would be a good time to tell him about Arizona State. I took a deep breath. I wiped my palms on the skirt of my dress, strangely nervous. Why was I so worried to tell Michael my good news?

"Hmm..." Michael said when I was finished speaking. "That sounds really exciting, Bliss."

Warm relief flooded through me as he placed his hand on top of mine. He was cool as porcelain.

"Before you make any final decisions though, you should keep something in mind," he said. "You might only spend a year there before you find yourself wrapped up in, oh, future plans."

He smiled enigmatically and brushed my hair from my face. He pulled me close and kissed me hard, causing that familiar rush of heat between my legs. I kept my eyes open while we kissed, studying his face.

It was obvious what he meant by future plans. Michael wanted us to get married. He wanted me to be his perfect society bride and make his perfect society home. Those things would come before softball. Part of me wanted all that too, wanted to be convinced. But I wouldn't make it easy for him by putting the words in his mouth. He needed to say them himself.

Chapter 19

Thwap. Snag. Thwap. Snag. Thwap. Snag.

The tennis ball bounced hard as I hurled it at the brick wall.

Thwap. Snag. Thwap. Snag. Thwap. Snag.

I threw it harder and higher, sending the ball wild and scooping and stretching to catch it.

In five hours, we would play our first game of the tournament. It would set the tone for the rest of our time. Either we would win and establish the upper hand, or we would lose and have to fight from behind for the victory. Losing wasn't an option.

Thwap. Snag. Thwap. Snag. Thwap. Snag.

My breathing came hard. I missed the ball as it sailed high and hard over my right shoulder. Someone behind me caught it.

I put my hands on my knees, bent over, and caught my breath, my lungs burned with exertion.

"You'll run yourself ragged before the game," Chris said.

I didn't turn around. "I'll be fine. I'll be loose. I need to shut my brain off so I can focus better."

I held my hand out for the ball. Instead of giving it to me, she chucked it at the wall. I twisted to the left to snag it.

"Let's play then," Chris said.

I hesitated. Chris wasn't wearing a glove. It was only a tennis ball, but I didn't want to hurt her. I threw it tentatively at the brick. Chris didn't return the courtesy. She fired the ball low and fast at the wall. I had to dive to catch it. Her smile asked me why I was holding back when she definitely wasn't.

I shrugged and aimed the ball directly in front of Chris. It whipped back at her face. She put both hands up and caught it neatly. Without hesitation, she pitched it right back and I caught it.

We fell into a rhythm, silent except the sound of the ball slapping off the wall.

Thwap. Snag. Thwap. Snag. Thwap. Snag. Thwap. Snag. Thwap. Snag. Thwap. Snag.

There was no set time or rules for our game. If one of us missed, we just started up again. Time melted away until we were both sweaty and flushed. I was pleased to see Chris breathing heavy. We sweated it out every day, Chris never actually did the drills.

We carried on for a while longer until Chris held up a hand for me to stop. Her short hair was mussed, and her temples shone with sweat. Her exertion softened her.

"I'm not in the same shape I used to be," she said. "That's it for me this morning."

"Sometimes I feel like I could just play and play forever," I said, and then cringed, realizing that might come off insulting to Chris.

She tidied her hair back into place, watching me the whole time.

"You could, you know. You could make it your life. I have."

Her words filled me with lightness. Maybe there was a chance I could have a life dedicated to softball. This tournament didn't have to be it for me. Out of habit, my eyes slid to her left ring finger again. Empty. Of course. I already knew that. Why should I think that you could have a husband and a career that took you all over the country? A familiar weight settled on my chest. I met Chris's gaze. She'd caught me checking her marital status.

"It's lonely though, isn't it?" I asked. May as well push my luck.

"Yes, it can be. But I'm mostly happy with my choices. No one comes to pick me up after practice and take me out for dinner. But no one expects me to have dinner on the table for him either," she said and turned to leave. Conversation over. "See you in a bit, Bliss. Good work."

I stood alone with the tennis ball in hand. No one was here now to stop me from playing. What would a lifetime of that be like? I threw the ball at the wall again.

Thwap. Snag. Thwap. Snag. Thwap. Snag.

Chapter 20

"Bennet on deck!" Jem read from the lineup.

Like I needed the reminder. I was already on my feet, prowling the dugout. My skin crawled with nerves. I willed my stomach to stop its somersaults. It was the first inning of the first game. The sharp tang of freshly cut ballpark grass filled the air and the sun beat down on us. We'd gone out and stopped them in the field, now we needed to prove ourselves at bat.

Jem put his hand on my shoulder and left it there momentarily. I let the warmth spread through my body.

"You're fine," he said. He whirled me around to meet my eyes. "Look at me. You're bugging and it's not like you. Take a deep breath. You're going to get out there and you're going to take as many pitches as possible. See what she's got. That's it."

"You mean, check out your new girlfriend?" I said. I'd calmed down enough to crack a joke, but missed Jem's touch when he took his hand away.

"She's not my type," he said.

I exhaled a breath I didn't realize I was holding. I didn't have the guts to ask him what his type was. Anyway, why did I even care? Jem was awful and I already had a boyfriend.

"Bennet, I wanna see a dinger out there," Coach said and slapped me on the back. "And listen to Jem. I want you to watch this girl."

Damn. No swinging on the first pitch.

I stepped into the on deck circle with the warm up bat and willed all superficial thoughts away. The stands were packed with spectators waving tiny American flags. Their cheers and applause faded to a low background hum. Clear your mind, clear your mind, Bliss. I warmed up my swing and watched Valentina take on Karen. Karen was behind in the count. Even though baseball was a team sport, so much of it came down to a contest of wills between hitter and pitcher. It was a battle of skill and psychology. The best hitters didn't just have good form, they could read pitchers in a way that made them reveal all their secrets without letting on that they knew anything at all.

This time, Karen came out ahead. She managed to slap a single off a high fastball on the inside. Instead of watching the play, I kept my eyes on Valentina's fox face. How did she take getting beat? Did it shake her at all?

Her face was stone. Not a single tell. I was up.

"Here's the easy out I've been waiting for," she said as I jogged to the plate.

Was she joking? I expected a little quiet trash talk from the catcher, but the pitcher actually yelling something to the hitter? I turned to the umpire. He put both his hands up.

"Let's just play ball ladies," he barked.

I zeroed in on Valentina. Her eyes were narrowed into slits as she considered the call. I shifted my focus to her core. Eyes could lie, but the body told the truth. All I wanted to do was watch. I'd have to fight my natural instincts to swing immediately, but this time Jem was right — it wouldn't do me any good to get a hit off the first pitch. I needed to experience as many throws as possible.

Valentina tensed up and delivered. A fat meatball, straight down the middle. She knew I wasn't going to swing at the first one and used the opportunity to get a strike on the board. Damn Jem. Regret flickered in my chest but I shook it off. A nice hit now wouldn't help me in the long run.

The next two came in low and outside. She was trying to get me to chase the ball down, but I wasn't having it. I stood statue-still, my bat frozen.

"Way to watch em, Bennet!" Someone yelled from the stands.

I met Valentina's eyes. Go ahead, put on a show. She stared me down, shook off her catcher's call. She wound up. Inside fastball. Strike.

Two strikes, two balls. I shifted impatiently and looked to Coach for permission. He nodded. I swung on the next pitch. Too slow, I sent it wild and foul. It was still two and two. Valentina released and I heaved a mighty swing… and popped the ball up. It was caught easily by the shortstop.

Inning over. I trotted back to the dugout for my glove and tried not to let the humiliation show. It wasn't technically Valentina's promised strikeout, but it was pretty close.

"You'll get her next time, kid," Coach said.

"Yeah, yeah," I said. "She's good, but she's not that good."

Good was on the mound now. Linda fanned the girls. I didn't even need to lift my glove once. She really made our job that easy.

Unfortunately, Valentina answered by making quick work of us. The game was still scoreless going into the fourth. Karen passed around the tub of Double Bubble and instructed us all the to take some with the same authority she used behind the plate.

"Chewing helps," she said. "Things are turning around for us now."

"Bennet up first," Jem said.

Linda had managed to strike out three in a row again. As she'd say, she was en fuego.

I carefully eased on my batting glove, took a few practice swings and stepped to the plate. Valentina raised one eyebrow at me.

Back for more? Her eyes asked.

You're damn right I am. This time, I'd smack anything that came straight down the plate.

But she wasn't going to give it to me easy on the first pitch. She knew that's what I wanted after last time. That's what I'd be waiting for. The throw blazed in low and outside. I watched it roll by, stepped away from the plate as the ump called it a ball.

I watched her body straighten out in preparation for the next pitch. Her eyes narrowed, she nodded slightly. I tightened up my grip. My ball was coming, I knew it.

Time slowed down. I saw the flare of her nostrils before her wind up. The twist of her body. The pink shoelace tied around her wrist. And I watched that ball every millisecond of its journey. It was like she'd tossed a beach ball my way. I stepped into the pitch, engaged the core Chris had been busting us to strengthen and swung with everything I had. The bat vibrated as the ball smacked off the sweet spot. The ball flew off the bat and sailed into the outfield, past the center fielder's outstretched glove and over the fence.

Time sped up again as Team USA's roar filled my ears. I dropped the bat and loped around the bases, my cheeks hurting from smiling so hard.

My homer was the end of our drought. Like a dam bursting open, we drove in hit after hit. Valentina's confidence seemed shaken, as even our weakest hitters managed to lob off singles. Only their stellar defence was able the staunch the bleeding.

The game ended at the top of the seventh, after we held them scoreless throughout at 6-0. The ump called it, and I walked back to the dugout in a daze. Did that really just happen? Could it be that easy?

"We did it!" Karen screamed and I gave myself over to the wild happiness of the moment.

"USA! USA! USA!" We chanted, knotted together tightly.

Even Coach and Chris joined in. But where was Jem? He belonged with us even if he was a sourpuss. I broke away from the pack, held out my arm to pull him into the circle, but he shrugged off my welcome.

"Everyone needs to calm down. You're getting too far ahead of yourselves. You haven't won the whole thing yet. And overconfidence is the quickest way to fail," he said, loud enough for everyone to hear.

His words were an unwanted cold shower. The smile dropped off my face.

"Way to be a fun sucker," Nancy said.

Jem wasn't bothered. "Look at them, do you think they're beat?"

Inside the Soviet dugout, despair hadn't broken out. The coaches were stoic, the girls calm. They didn't act like they'd just been whooped. They were taking us in. Valentina met my eyes, nodded. They reminded me of our old Persian cat, Lady, when she was playing with a mouse. Lady liked to see what the critter could do before going in for the kill. It was almost like they knew something we didn't know. It gave me the chills.

They weren't beat at all. And there was no way the second win would come as easy as the first.

Chapter 21

The Team U.S.A. dorm was at a fever pitch after our win. Someone had brought a radio and cranked up the volume on a Top 20 station. The twins were practising new cheers in the hallway. We talked loudly to be heard over the ruckus.

"I'm going to eat that egg," Becca said.

Jane sighed. "It really isn't a real egg, Becs."

I was uneasy. I couldn't shake Jem's words or the way the Soviet team took their loss.

Nancy grabbed me by the wrist. She clutched a copy of the latest Vogue.

"Bliss, come here. I want your take on this dress. Oscar de la Renta, new collection. Do you like it? I know it's last minute, but I'm thinking of swapping the deb dress I have now for this one."

She thrust the glossy magazine in my hands. Annoyance flared up. Debut dresses were the last thing on my mind and I was sick of Nancy's constant bragging. But I didn't want to start a fight. Not tonight while everyone was so happy.

"I'll come to see it later. I promised Peggy I would call her after our game. She's dying to know what happened," I said.

Nancy pouted. "I'm sure she already knows. I mean, it was on the news after all. God, could Chris be any butcher in that tracksuit? She should invest in a little lipstick."

Why did Nancy need to constantly insult Chris, who had gotten us in game shape so we could win. I was done playing nice.

"I'll see you later," I said and strode away.

I suddenly desperately needed to talk to Peggy. It didn't take long to find a payphone.

"Why does Nancy have to be like that? I don't care what designer dress she's wearing to the ball, but she's obsessed with bragging to me all the same. I mean, we're all wearing designer dresses. It's the Cotillion Ball for chrissakes. Who would show up in anything less?" I said, venting my frustration.

Peggy laughed in reply.

"Cut her some slack Bliss. She's not bragging, she's looking for your approval."

I was shocked into silence. There's no way that's why Nancy always acted like a huge snob around me.

"What planet are you from? That is not what is going on."

Peggy sighed. Papers rustled in the background. She was probably making a seating plan or whatever crazy detail she had left for her wedding and was tired of playing referee. I dropped it.

"Anyway, it's fine. I'll ignore her," I said. "Did I tell you we won today? I hit a homer!"

"I know! We set up a phone tree to get results. Great job, Bliss."

The operator cut into the line in a tinny recorded voice. "To continue your conversation, please insert 10 cents."

I searched my pockets for more coins. Nothing.

"Shit, I'm sorry Peggy. I have to go."

"To continue your conversation, please insert 10 cents."

"That's fine. I love you, Bliss. And give Nancy a break. She could use it — "

Click. The line went dead. Heartless phone company.

Ugh, Nancy. But Mama would probably love it if I were as excited about the deb ball. If I went to Arizona, the only balls I'd get near to would be softballs. Was I going to be okay with that?

Maybe I should go back and pretend as if I cared about Nancy's dumb dress.

I found her flipping through Vogue on her bunk.

"Hey," I said. "Peggy says hi."

"Oh hi," she sniffed. "You know, I'm not sure about that dress anymore. I remembered that Ella Greenwood is wearing something similar. I wouldn't want Bobby Rice to mix us up and start following me around like a puppy dog."

Ah, there was the Nancy I knew and couldn't stand.

"Why are you so mean sometimes?" I asked.

Nancy narrowed her eyes.

"I'm not. I'm just being honest."

Which was more than you could say for me.

I trudged down the hallway to my room, but the screams and the laughter from the other girls grated on my nerves. I needed to be alone.

I found my way to the roof and gulped in deep, greedy breaths when the fresh air hit my face. The campus was so peaceful at night. I wanted to just curl up and quietly think under the stars. But I wasn't alone.

His movements caught my eye first. Jem was in the far corner of the roof, shadowboxing. His fists flew as he fought invisible enemies. He was shirtless in his baseball pants and sweat dripped down his muscular chest.

I watched, fascinated. His face held me as he jabbed and crossed, deked and uppercut. Jem's eyes were raw anger. This was different from his usual surly expression. His face was pure rage. I'd never seen anything like it.

I should have slunk away before he could catch me. Instead, I crept forward, drawn by his movement. He was wild like he could keep punching until he just collapsed. I needed to stop him.

Slowly, quietly, I approached. When I within arm's reach, I gently placed my hand on his shoulder.

A flurry of movement and pain blossomed hot and fierce on my cheek. Instantly, I was on the ground, tears streaming from my eyes.

"Bliss, I am so sorry," Jem said. He hovered over me. Whatever anger had been there was completely drained from his face. Instead, he was anxious, examining my cheek.

"You hit me," I said. What the hell had just happened?

"I know. God, I'm so sorry. I would never hurt you. Let me go down and get you some ice. What are you doing out here?" His voice quavered. The softness had returned to his eyes and they glinted with tears.

What the hell was wrong with him? That was more frightening than what might happen to my face. I touched my cheek experimentally. If I were lucky, it wouldn't bruise. Mama would just die if I wound up with a shiner, and who knows what Michael would do.

"What am I doing out here? What are you doing? You looked like you were trying to kill someone. Who were you pretending to hit?"

He let out a ragged breath.

"Mr. Fredrick," he said.

The gym teacher?

"For failing you?" I asked, incredulous.

"No. For something much worse," he replied.

I wanted to ask more, but his face told me to leave it. He carried himself like a beaten dog. There was something so scared and haunted about him, that it would be cruel to drag it out. Best to leave him to wrestle with his demons alone on the rooftop.

I patted his hand.

"Well take it easy, killer. I'm not sure how many more headshots I can take," I said, trying to lighten the moment.

"Bliss, I —" he said.

He wanted to apologize again. But the ache in my cheek was already receding. It would disappear, but Jem wouldn't soon forget the pain he had inflicted.

"I know," I said. "I forgive you."

He hung his head, rubbing his hand over his bristly short hair.

"It's just that, can you maybe not mention this to anyone? I know some of the parents already have a problem with me here..." He didn't finish his thought.

"Because you're black," I said.

"I was going to say because I'm a delinquent," Jem replied.

I blushed, embarrassed that I had pointed out the color of his skin.

"But you're not wrong," Jem said. "Elmhurst likes to call itself progressive, but it's just as bad as the rest of the country."

"I'm sorry," I said. I didn't know what else to say. Jem's problems were ones that I didn't even know how to begin wrestling with. He probably wouldn't think much of my insignificant issues.

I got up and walked away, leaving him with the sweat cooling on his chest in the night air. Jem stayed where he was, staring out at the darkened rooftop.

Chapter 22

The day after the game was a free day. Sort of. Since we weren't playing, Chris used the time to take us into the practice field and drill us for hours.

We were unfocused, scattered, and still high off our W yesterday. Everyone thought the next win would come easy. I wasn't so sure.

"Fine, since I can't get you to concentrate on fielding, we're going to tee up some BP," Chris said.

For the next hour, we all took turns at bat, knocking out 50 balls apiece.

Midway through Nancy's turn, the Soviets jogged by. They ran in perfect formation, making two neat rows behind their coach, who rode a bike.

"I saw them out there before we started," Jane said. "They've been at it for at least two hours."

They did a loop closer to us. While their form was perfect, they were visibly strained. Kata was huffing and Valentina's sharp face had turned cherry red from exertion.

When they got to the far end of the field they stopped, doubled over. The Soviet coach barked something at them, and they straightened up and started off again.

"They're putting on a show," Chris said. "And a good one at that. Note the discipline. That's how they'll get us, you know, the discipline."

"That girl's barely holding it together," Jane said.

A straggler at the end of the line had broken formation. Each sluggish step was labored. As they got closer, I could make out her face clearly. Jane was right, the girl was at her limit. Her blonde hair was darkened with sweat. Instead of being flushed from the effort, she was a ghostly white.

The girl staggered and seemed close to falling, but straightened herself with great effort. Now she was really behind the pack. The coach noticed and rode back to catch up with her. Good, he would see that she wasn't doing well. That girl needed to stop before she passed out.

Instead, he yelled something and gave her a shove at the small of the back. The girl pumped her arms, tried to pick up speed to catch up with the group. Tears streaked down her cheeks. What the hell? That wasn't right. Chris shook her head in disapproval. My anxiety grew as the girl struggled. She was going to get hurt. She was hurting.

"Say something," I said before I realized what I was doing. "We can't just watch him bully her until she collapses."

"It's not our place to judge another's coaching technique," Chris said, her lips pressed into a thin white line.

Whatever honor code she followed was more important to her than stepping in. It was so stupid.

I closed my eyes to will it all away, like that time I saw a man beating a puppy in an alley off Main Street. I yelled at him to stop but he just laughed and walked toward me. I was all alone, so I just ran, sobbing all the way home. I called Daddy at work and he sent one of his guys to find the puppy. They told me that the dog had been checked out at the vet and he was fine. But I heard Daddy talking to Mama late at night when they thought I was asleep. "It was gruesome," Daddy said. I pressed my eyes shut and buried those words deep down inside me where I didn't have to hear them or think about them.

I turned to Coach. He crossed his arms and spat out some chew, in silent agreement with Chris.

Jem was agitated by the scene.

"Coach," Jem said, calling out to the Soviet leader. "You have one on the end there who could use a timeout."

I smiled at him, relieved he was speaking out. That someone was doing something.

"You presume to tell me what to do," the Russian coach said. He was an imposing man, with cruel eyes and a large bristly mustache.

The Soviet girls had stopped running, and he screamed at them to keep going.

Jem bristled. "Not presuming, sir, just concerned for the well-being of one of your team members."

"My team members are fine. Please concern yourself with your own undisciplined team. My girls listen to me and trust me to always know what is best."

With a final blow to his whistle, he peddled off.

Jem clenched his fists. "That son of a bitch."

"Easy, son," Coach said, placing a hand on his arm, but Jem shook him off in frustration.

The other team continued its laps around the park. The straggler got further and further behind until she was closer to us and our practice field than the rest of her team. Mustache yelled something else at her. She took a few more steps and then someone shut off the lights. Her knees buckled and she crumpled into the field like a rag doll.

Jem grabbed a bottle of water and sprinted to the girl's side.

"Jane, go get a doctor," he yelled over his shoulder.

I ran behind him, straining to catch up. Jem gently propped her up and checked her breathing.

"She's overheated," he said and unzipped her jacket. Then he opened up the water bottle and slowly poured the cool liquid over her face, rubbing it into her sweaty hair.

The girl spluttered and came to, spitting out water. I let out a breath I didn't realize I was holding.

"*Kto ty*?" She asked, dazed.

"I don't know what that means, honey. I'm Jem from Team U.S.A. You were running and then you collapsed," he said.

"*Chto?*"

Jem smoothed her hair. "It's okay, just relax. A doctor is coming."

He offered her the rest of the water and she took long, greedy gulps from the bottle.

Our team had formed a circle around the girl and Jem.

"Hey now," Jem said. "Let's give her some space."

Reluctantly we backed up. But I was grateful for the room when the Soviet coach stalked toward us, furious.

"Did I not just tell you not to interfere with my players? Are you Americans really as dumb as they say you are, boy?"

Jem stood, his eyes ablaze. "Listen asshole. I'm sure you can abuse your players as much as you want back home where no one cares, but in America, you can't treat people like that. You don't treat people like that."

He had slowly crept toward the Russian coach, his fists sticks of dynamite, ready to blow at his sides. The vein on his forehead bulged.

"You think you're a big man?" Jem shouted. "Does it make you feel powerful to treat girls like that? Do you? You want to pick on someone, how about me?"

Jem shoved the coach in the chest. The Russian's eyes bulged. He muttered an incomprehensible curse. Icy fear gripped my chest. Were they going to fight? The Russian had at least 50 pounds on Jem. And he was mean.

"Okay, whoa, whoa. Easy there," Coach said and stepped between them. Relief eased my knot of tension.

He pulled Jem away from the crowd, murmuring reassuring things in his ear. Gradually, Jem's breathing evened out.

"Well, I think we've seen all we need to here for today," Chris said. "You're all dismissed. Curfew is at 10 and I expect to see everyone at breakfast."

Coach was still with Jem, talking him down. I wanted to go to Jem, to comfort him. Unexpectedly, I ached to hold him and soothe him. But I didn't know what I would say. Or why he reacted the way he did. What was he thinking? I didn't stay to find out. I had a date with Michael and I could use the extra time to get ready. Tonight, I wanted to be pretty for him. I would actually be able to wash my hair and if I got lucky I could get Cher to do it for me.

"Ooh, your hair so gorgeous. I could spend all night playing with it," Cher said later in her room. "Tada!"

She snapped her bubblegum and thrust a hand mirror at me. My normally limp ponytail had been transformed into flowing copper waves. The top half had been teased into a bouffant, and a blue patterned headband to match my minidress completed the do. Cher's expertly applied makeup transformed me into a confident woman. I glimpsed the future version of myself, someone who went to the salon instead of the ballpark.

"Wow," I said.

"I know. Michael will swallow his tongue when he sees you," she replied.

I hoped so.

"Wow," Michael said when he picked me up, echoing my word. "Babes, you look incredible. I almost don't even want to take you out for dinner."

He appraised me from under heavy lids. He looked pretty incredible himself. His slicked dark hair accentuated his cheekbones, his tailored suit perfectly showed off his lean body.

"Thank you," I murmured, stepping forward to kiss him.

Instead of a quick peck, he pulled me in tight and kissed me passionately, pressing me up against the car. Heat flooded through me.

"Michael," I said, managing to break away, slightly out of breath. "You're going to mess my hair."

He flashed a devilish grin. "It's worth it, don't you agree?"

Michael opened the door for me and I slid in the front seat.

"Where are we going?" I asked as he pulled away from the dorm.

"You'll see," he said.

He placed his hand on my thigh, slowly moving it upwards until it was under my skirt.

I blushed, shifted in my seat.

"Michael," I said in a strangled voice.

But he didn't stop. As he kept his eyes on the road, he moved higher up my leg. I gasped. He grinned.

"I have a very special night planned for us," he said.

Chapter 23

I was coiled tight like a spring, ready to burst when Michael pulled up in front of Chez Amis. "You want to eat here?" I asked. Michael didn't even like French food. But he did like to show off by eating at expensive restaurants.

"They have the best escargot in town," he said, opening the door for me.

I was still flushed, distracted me from the fact that escargot was a snail and there was no way in hell was eating one of those slimy suckers.

"Oh, um, you didn't want to go somewhere else first?" I asked.

How unladylike of me. How easy it was to forget all the rules.

Michael just smiled. He liked the way I was the one left wanting more for once.

"Why, Bliss, are you in a rush to go somewhere?"

My cheeks warmed. "I just thought that we might want to continue the discussion we were having in the car."

I gasped as he grabbed me from the waist and pulled me in tight for a kiss so hard I bent over backwards. My head spun. I had never wanted Michael more than I did then. It was like I was 15 again before we had even started dating. When Michael was just a dreamy senior I thought I was so in love with I could barely stay conscious in his presence.

"Later," he promised through ragged breaths.

"Ahem," the Maître D said, clearing his throat. "May I show you to your seats?"

I sat across from Michael at a small, candlelit table in front of the window.

"Isn't this nice?" He said, smirking.

Underneath the table, his hand was on my knee, moving up and stroking my inner thigh. Every touch was like fire and I had to bite down on my bottom lip to keep from moaning.

"Now, what shall we order?" Michael asked, making a grand show of unfurling the menu while keeping one hand underneath the table.

But instead of reading, he was distracted by someone at another table. His teasing hand came off my leg to rake through his hair.

"Is that Jeff Somers? What the hell is he doing here with that foreign-looking man?"

I craned my neck to see.

"Don't stare Bliss!"

Michael threw his napkin down in anger. His face was dangerous.

"I'm going to see what this is all about."

I waited for him, playing with my napkin. The spell was broken. My legs were cold without the heat from Michael's hand.

He exchanged a few words with the man and stormed back to the table.

"Foreign buyer. I knew it. Somers, the bastard, had a deal with my family if it ever came to that. I need to tell Father what's going on. I swear, if everyone only thinks of himself, this whole industry will be sold piecemeal to God knows who."

With that, Michael was off on his favorite topic: foreign ownership of American steel interests. His cheeks flushed and his eyes lit up when he spoke. He barely paused for breath when the waiter appeared and only gave a short, sharp order. He was completely caught up in his true passion. Changes in the steel industry affected my family as well, but I didn't think about it. I didn't even care. I didn't associate Daddy's wealth with any kind of industry fluctuations. It was just always there. Would the steel industry ever interest me?

Michael droned on as I nodded and hummed occasionally. These days, we just took turns talking at each other about things we were interested in while the other person listened. Was it wrong that we didn't actually have a conversation? But I guess it was expected that men and women have different tastes. Mama had taught me that the most powerful thing a woman could do for a man was to make him feel heard. And not bother him too much with silly problems.

The food came and Michael picked through his meal. So did I. The fatty, heavy cuisine did nothing for me. And I didn't want to have to run the cream off at practice tomorrow.

Eventually, Michael wound down. It was my chance to fish for information about something that had been nagging at me.

"I saw Jem doing something strange yesterday," I said and quickly related the scene on the roof, leaving out the part where Jem hit me. Thank God there wasn't a bruise. Michael wouldn't care for that much.

"He said he was pretending to hit Mr. Frederick, who had done something worse than fail him. What did he mean by that?" I asked.

I held my breath for an answer. Suddenly, I absolutely needed to know.

Michael put down his napkin. "Fredrick is a good old boy who isn't shy about how he feels about negroes. Jem mouthed off to him after class and Frederick took off his belt and tried to whip him, called him the n-word and everything. Winston Everest's younger brother told us all about it. That's why Jem stopped going to gym class. I thought everyone knew."

"I didn't know!" I said. The fatty food heaved in my stomach. The thought of the gym teacher hating Jem for the skin he was born with made me completely sick. I had to rein my imagination in and force myself to not picture the scene. Jem would never want my pity.

"Yes, well, we try to shield you from the worst of the world," Michael said, leaning forward to pat my hand. "And this is why babe. You're a little green around the gills."

"He should have reported him," I insisted.

"Then he'd have to explain why he was fighting with a teacher. Besides, Mr. Frederick is a war hero. They weren't going to put him out based on one student's complaint."

My jaw dropped in disbelief. Was that really why Jem hadn't said anything? Choosing to flunk out instead of going to class because no one would take his side? In a flash, Jem's attitude made perfect sense. I'd resent the hell out of the Lady Scarlets too. He should have been spending his time practising his own game, not helping us with ours. Instead, he was being punished for being a victim. It was so goddamn unfair.

I wasn't sure what to make of Coach. On one hand, it was a very generous Coach-like thing to help Jem out of a jam by making him our assistant coach. On the other hand, why the hell didn't he speak up for him? If we could all turn a blind eye to hate in our own school we weren't much better than those Soviets mindlessly following authority, letting that coach run his player until she collapsed.

While I was brooding, Michael paid the bill.

"Follow me," he said.

I walked blankly behind him, numb from shock and disgust.

I didn't notice it earlier, but the restaurant was in the base of a hotel. Michael took my hand and led me to the elevator.

"Where are we going?" I asked.

Michael dangled a key in response. "I told you I had a special night planned out for us."

Inside our room, rose petals had been sprinkled in a path leading to the bed and champagne chilled on ice. Lit candles flickered throughout. Michael must have had help setting this up.

"What are we celebrating?" I asked.

"Us," he said simply.

"But it's not our anniversary," I said.

"Do we really need an excuse for an evening like this?"

Michael strode toward me and pushing my hair aside, kissed my neck. This time, I tingled with more than desire. His hands felt safe. It was nice to be touched the way he ran hands over me, caressing me like a delicate item. My numbness melted away. With Michael it was right. He was the kind of boy you were supposed to do this with. We kissed deeply and I let him lead me to the bed.

I sat on the edge, my heart pounding as I watched him undress. He shed his clothing slowly, unbuttoning his shirt with deliberate movements, revealing his taut torso. He stood before me in just his briefs. He was beautiful.

"Come here," he said. "I'll never let anything bad happen to you. You know that?"

He unzipped my dress and I stood before him in my frothy black slip.

We'd been here before. I wasn't sure if I wanted to go all the way, but at a certain point, it just became expected. How could I say no after Michael had gone to all this trouble? The dinner and the hotel suite couldn't have been cheap. At a certain point, a girl can get a reputation for being frigid. And that's almost as bad as being a slut.

"This time, I'm ready," I said.

I wasn't really. As soon as I said it, I knew I didn't want to. But there was no real going back now. I'd already said yes, and I couldn't just say no once I had. Besides, this was my boyfriend. I'd wanted to for so long with him. Now he had made the perfect night for me to lose my virginity. All I had to do was enjoy it. This is how nice girls lost it. After a romantic evening with their gorgeous boyfriends.

I lied back on the bed and it occurred to me that I'd never asked if Michael were a virgin. He sure didn't act like one. But Mama said it was only important that a girl stayed a virgin until she was married. It seemed like men could do whatever they wanted.

Was Jem still a virgin? Did he have a girlfriend that he took out for expensive dinners and then brought out to hotel rooms? What was his body like under his clothes? He was broader than Michael, taller too with longer limbs. While Michael was lithe, Jem was all brawn. His large muscles bulged under his baseball shirts. I would be light as a ragdoll in his arms.

I closed my eyes and pictured Jem's dark skin and warm brown eyes. Now Jem was the one kissing me, the one I wanted. I could almost smell him, that crisp hint of freshly cut grass. Jem, Jem, Jem. I bit my lip to keep his name inside but I was overwhelmed with feeling.

"Oh, Je-"

Michael stiffened and stopped. I opened my eyes, cold water to my senses. The spell was broken. I had to admit the truth to myself: I wasn't in Jem's strong arms, I was here with Michael.

"What are you saying?" He asked, eyes narrow with suspicion.

"Gently," I gasped my cheeks flushed more with embarrassment than desire.

Satisfied, Michael went back to nuzzling my neck. I willed my mind somewhere far away and I gave myself over to touch and taste.

I was no longer a virgin.

"Groovy," Michael said.

I kissed him primly and excused myself to go to the bathroom. Alone, I cooled my flushed face against the porcelain wall tiles.

Losing my virginity should have been the most special, intimate moment of my life. Instead, I had spent the entirety of the experience fantasizing about another man. Where had that even come from? I blushed hotly. I didn't really see Jem like that. At least, I didn't think I did. How could I ever face him again, after what I had just done with him in mind? Goddammit. I should have just stuck to baseball. That was something I knew about for sure, at least.

I splashed water on my face and pressed a wet cloth to my neck. And what about Michael? I could never tell anyone who had really been on my mind. Now that I'd given Michael what he wanted, I couldn't risk losing him and being labelled used goods. What would everyone think of me then? Losing my virginity had sealed the deal, I was Michael's forever.

"We should head out soon," I said when I calmed down enough to come out of the bathroom. I tried to keep my voice light and cheery even though my hands shook slightly. "You know how Coach is about curfew. He'll tan my ass if I don't make it back."

Michael frowned. "But I wanted to keep you here longer. I do have the hotel room all night."

I tried not to cringe at the implication.

"I know, I want to too, but I'm dead meat if I miss curfew. Next time, we'll plan it so I can stay overnight."

Michael perked up at the mention of next time.

"Alright, I'll take you back. You're lucky I'm patient with all this softball nonsense. Other guys wouldn't be so okay with having girlfriends busier and sportier than them."

He's right, I am lucky he's so accommodating.

"You're sweet," I say. "Anyway, the tournament will be over in just a week."

Michael kissed me on the forehead. "And then you'll be free to start working on our real future together."

My smile was tight. Michael had made it perfectly clear: If I chose Arizona, he would no longer be putting up with me.

Chapter 24

It was game two day, and I banned all thoughts of the night before into a deep, dark corner my mind. Now was the time to focus. A flicker of embarrassment rose up when Jem sat next to me at the breakfast table. His arm brushed against mine as he reached for the hot rolls and I flinched at his touch.

Hurt flashed across his face.

"Bliss, you know that I'm sorry, right?" He lowered his voice, eyes pleading with mine. "It was an accident. I just so caught up in my own thing, that I didn't... I would never intentionally hurt you."

I couldn't remember the last time someone cared so much about what I thought.

"Why didn't you ever report Mr. Fredericks to the principal?" I asked.

Jem chewed his food in silence. "What difference would it have made?" He eventually asked.

I tried to imagine a gym teacher trying to lay a hand on me. He'd be out on his ass before lunch period was over.

"To get him fired!" I said.

Jem scoffed. "And then what? Do you think he'd like me more? Would losing his job make him see me as a human being instead of a whipping boy? You think he'd thank me for that? Nah."

He shook his head. "Better to just stay the hell out of his way, go about my own business and leave him far behind," Jem said.

"But you failed gym because of it," I said. "I just don't understand why—"

Jem cut me off.

"No, you wouldn't understand. And count your lucky stars for that. Because you wouldn't want to live your life like me, wondering if someone is going to hate you or want to hurt you because of how you were born. Your skin color gives you freedom. Mine just makes me cautious," he said.

"I don't know how free I am," I shot back, thinking of all the unwritten rules that guided my life.

Jem finished his coffee in one glug.

"You're a fool if you can't see it," he said and strode away.

I watched him leave, scrambled eggs cooling on my plate. My orange juice tasted sour in my mouth. I felt ashamed that my problems seemed so petty in comparison and resentful to Jem for making me see them that way. I pushed my plate aside, appetite shot. It was time to get game ready.

The team was quiet on the way to the diamond. Nobody wanted to even breath the hope that rattled around Big Bertha: If we won today, we'd win the whole thing. Instead, we strode silently, in sync. The whites of our Team USA jerseys gleamed in the blinding mid-morning sunlight. Spectators continued to stream in, holding signs and flags, chatting happily and lining up for concession fries. Their laughter filled the air and I envied their enjoyment. My stomach was ready to rebel. The heat of the past two days had baked the dirt in the park, sending up clouds of dust as we tramped through.

"Someone ought to spray that down. How can the umps make a call if the whole pitch is a dustbowl?" Jane asked.

As if on cue, the ground staff came out to groom the diamond. They sprayed and raked, making neat lines in the dirt and rolling out the perfect chalk lines. I tried to appreciate the care that went into getting the ballpark ready for the game. This could be the last time I got to kick up the dirt in a pristine field. I wanted to win, badly. But I also wasn't ready to say goodbye to this feeling yet.

We stretched quietly in front of the dugout as Coach went through his usual pre-game wind-up. The heat of the day was getting to him and he used an old handkerchief to sop up the sweat from his brow. The bleachers were full and the guys in the booth were playing that Eagles song about taking it easy over the loudspeakers. Easier said than done.

The Soviets marched into their first-base dugout in perfect unison. The familiar pre-game butterflies tickled in my stomach. I forced myself to take deep, calming breaths. I had no use for nerves. Softball was a sport for the level-headed.

"Alright kids, you've got em on the ropes here," said Coach, swiping at his forehead sweat. "Do not lose your focus. Just do it exactly like you did the other day. Play hard, have fun, go home champions. You with me?"

"Yeah!" We called back.

"That really wasn't loud enough. Jem, you hear that? I said... are you with me?!"

"YEAH!" We screamed back.

My heart pounded against my ribs. I bounced from foot to foot. We were away, so I was in the field first. I needed to chill out but stay sharp.

"Go, Bliss!" Someone called from the stands.

I followed the voice. Peggy was there with George, waving a sign. I waved back frantically. I wish she were out on the field with me, but seeing her friendly face eased my nerves.

I quickly traced my number in the dirt with my toe three times and then smoothed the ground back down. I was ready.

Linda threw out a few last warmup pitches. They seared over the plate and I smiled. Those were just a taste of what was to come. If they picked a tournament VIP, it should definitely be Linda.

The first batter got up and Linda took her down easily. She struck out looking on the fourth pitch.

"One up, one down," I called, beating the palm of my glove with my right fist.

The second batter also made no move to swing at the ball. She watched each pitch come in. Linda threw her some junk, baiting her into swinging. No luck. Instead, she also struck out looking.

I made the two down sign with my pinky and index finger. But that out was strange. It made sense to take a few throws off a new pitcher to see what she was made of, but everyone on that team had faced off against Linda. They already knew what she had.

Third up at the plate was a girl with short blond pigtails sticking out from underneath her helmet. She turned to her coach and gave a curt nod before stepping to the plate. She wriggled her hips and set her bat in the ready position.

Linda read a signal from Karen and gave the ok. She wound up, delivered, and... smack! The ponytailed girl smashed a hit off her bat. I bit my lip as it arced into the outfield, where Jane made a diving catch in right to get her out. Atta girl. Don't ever let anyone say girls in glasses can't play sports.

Applause burst from the stands. Jane stood up and brushed herself off, tossing the ball on the mound on her way to our dugout.

"Three up! Three down!" The girls cheered as we put on our batting gear, but I stayed quiet.

Something was off about the way that inning had gone down. Why had those two girls just stood and watched each ball come in only the have the next girl up play the first pitch perfectly? She must have gotten impatient watching her teammates at bat and gotten lucky. Maybe. But that wasn't a great answer either. The Reds having a hot day at the plate was the last thing I wanted.

"Alright kids, let's give em hell," Coach said and read the order. I was cleanup, as usual.

"It's the American Princess," Valentina called as I walked out to the plate, her thick accent dripping with sarcasm. "I think you will find it a new game today."

I was about to shoot back a smart answer when the umpire put up his hand. "None of that ladies. Let's keep this civil."

I tried to get back my cool while I got into my stance. There were two out and Becca was on first. The first pitch was a steamer coming high and outside. I went for it, slamming a line drive that the shortstop managed to get a piece of. She couldn't hold it, and the ball rolled into the field. Becca managed to turn two, but we were left stranded at first and third when Che popped out.

Shit.

Coach rallied us as we got our gloves. "Good start, good start. We're making em work for every out. I like that. Make them earn it."

I ran out to position for a whole new ballgame. The Soviets weren't just standing there watching anymore, they were swinging with full force and making contact. Our fielders were run ragged chasing balls down. By the time we made our third out, they had managed to score two runs.

Linda tried to shake it off, but their next turn at bat wasn't much of an improvement. They kept getting hits off her that she would've never given up before. Another run came in. Now the score was 3-0. What the hell? Had they studied game tape of Linda nonstop between our two games? How were they anticipating our every move? 3-0 was a pretty big hole. Not an insurmountable one, but we'd have to do some serious spadework if we were going to turn this game into anything more than a total write-off.

It didn't help that our offence wasn't coming close to matching theirs.

Valentina gave me a smirk and salute as I grounded out to the shortstop in the fourth inning. I would have given anything to wipe that smile off her face, but I had to admit she was good. Damn her.

Linda was in good shape in the next inning. She had the batter with a pitcher's count: one ball and two strikes. Now was Linda's time to start throwing junk. Part of Linda's talent was that she was a great actress. She could put something terrible over the plate and sell it down to the last second as a great throw.

This time was no different. Karen's signal called for the off-speed. The batter checked her dugout for instructions. Linda wound up, pitched, and then something unthinkable happened. The girl, sensing the ball wasn't coming in as fast, waited for an extra beat and then smacked the ball over Becca in center field with perfect timing. I winced. It was a goner. The score ratcheted up to 4-0.

Linda swore in Spanish. The word was hard and sharp under her breath. The twins stood in open-mouthed amazement. Something seriously fishy was going on. There was no way she could have known with total certainty that an off-speed was coming. No one, not even me, not even the best, ever managed to time it that perfectly. And yet this girl had. Maybe her coach had warned her it might be coming. Still, it's hard to resist your normal swing when it seems like a great pitch is coming your way.

Midway through the next up count, the batter's eyes were fixed on her dugout as well. It wasn't strange to look over before a turn at the plate for special instructions to bunt, but to constantly be checking in with the coach? Everyone else usually stared down the pitcher, getting into her head a little bit.

What was she looking at? Karen signalled to Linda, who nodded. The next pitch would be an outside fastball. The batter turned to the dugout, I followed her eyes to her coach, who gave her a complicated hand signal in return. She nodded in understanding.

This all happened in the fraction of time it took for Linda to prepare her next throw. And when it came, the girl was ready. She hammered a line drive to the left of me. Instinctively, I threw myself in its direction, stretching as far as my body would allow, straining to get my glove in place. I landed hard on my side and the breath whooshed out of me like a popped balloon. I lay still for a moment until Cher trotted over from second to check up on me.

"You okay?" She asked.

I got up in a daze clutching the ball. I'd made the catch. The crowd burst into applause but I barely registered the noise. My mind was swirling, struggling to connect what I had just seen and what had happened. It couldn't be, or could it? It was unheard of. That kind of trickery wouldn't be tolerated, even in the majors. It went against the baseball code of ethics.

"Time out," I croaked. I held my side, miming pain and limped to the dugout. It wasn't hard to fake injury. The bruises already blossomed across my ribs.

"Time!" Called the ump.

The team crowded around, trying to asses the damage.

"What's going on Bennet?" Coach asked. "I've seen you take harder falls than that."

"We need to switch the hand signals," I said, straightening up, signs of pain erased.

"What the hell are you talking about?" Coach said.

"I'll explain after the game. Just right now. We need to switch the signals. Reverse them. Something fast."

My voice took on a desperate edge. My teammates were puzzled. I knew I sounded bananas, but I just needed them to believe me. We didn't have time to get into my suspicions. I turned to Jem for support. Understanding seemed to have dawned on him. In the confusion, he took charge.

"Karen and Linda, do you still remember our signals from last year?"

"Sure," Karen said. "But they're kind of basic. Not as good as the ones we have now."

"Forget these ones. Use the olds ones. Got it? Linda, do you think you can handle that?"

The pitcher nodded grimly. "They're stealing signs, aren't they? *Taimados brujas.*"

Outrage rippled through our dugout.

"Don't worry about that right now," Jem said, making calming motions with his hands. "We'll sort it out later. Let's just get back out there and get it done. We can still win this game."

"Are you joking me? We're too deep in the hole," Nancy said.

I wish I didn't agree with her but she was right. We were drowning out there.

Jem cut his eyes toward her. "With an attitude like that, you'll get nothing done. It's not over until the last out. Let's concentrate on our game now. Crank those bats up and shut them down."

Nancy's gloom caught on. Their offence couldn't hammer us as bad without the tip-off for the pitch and our defence tightened up to shut them down. But we couldn't manage to catch up. We were cooked. The Reds held their lead and the game ended at the top of the seventh.

I was sick by the finish. Yesterday, victory seemed so close. The tiny hope that I nursed, the one that told me we could win and I could prove to everyone I was meant to play softball, dimmed. Why hadn't I hit a homerun? Or a grand slam? Surely, I could have done more to help us win. I should have noticed what was happening sooner! If only I'd trusted my instincts and realized something was wrong right away. Instead, I refused to believe the unthinkable. And it cost us. Now we were back on the ropes. We'd lost our lead in the tournament and were back to square one. The next game would be do or die. A sudden panic gripped my chest as I followed the rest of the team dejectedly into the changeroom.

Linda slammed her glove into the locker and screamed in frustration. Everyone started talking at once. We all wanted to know the same thing: What the hell just happened?

"How could they know our signals?" Karen asked Coach.

Jane answered instead.

"It's obvious, isn't it? One of us is a traitor."

Chapter 25

Jane's spy theory shocked everyone into silence.

"That's ridiculous," Chris said, trying to diffuse the situation.

She was cut off by Becca's squeals.

"What? A spy?? Someone here is a traitor?" She cried, clutching her glove. "I need to call my parents to see if they think it's still safe."

Everyone in the room started to babble at the same time. I wanted to roll my eyes at Becca's hysteria, but the other girls were grim. They actually seemed scared.

"Who was it?"

"What did she get?"

"Why did she do it?"

So many questions and not a single answer. The idea of one of us passing information was totally batshit. If I wanted to share national secrets, I wouldn't even know where to start. There are no people of international intrigue in our town. It's not like there's a Soviet Embassy down the block. Also, we're patriots in Elmhurst. Half the ladies in town are in Mama's Daughters of the American Revolution chapter. Not everyone loathes the Commies as much as Daddy does, but nobody likes them either. Or thinks that Communism is a good system. We're proud Americans. Everyone says that our 4th of July parade is one of the best in the state. A high school softball player from small-town Ohio moonlighting as a secret Soviet spy was total hogwash.

I told everyone just as much, but no one really listened. Something ugly had started to happen: We started to suspect each other. Sharon, our backup catcher, turned to Susie and Deb, eyes narrowed.

"Didn't your family go on a trip to Kyiv a few years ago?" She asked.

The team chattered at the revelation. The twins put their hands up in a unified sign of defence.

"It was for our brother's hockey tournament!" They said.

"Oh really," Sharon said. "Make any new friends while you were there? Didn't your brother's team end up losing?"

Her implication was clear: This wasn't the first time the Twins had faced the Soviets and came out losers. The silence was deadly, meant for Susie and Deb to drown in while they explained themselves. Deb's eyes welled with tears and Susie's mouth twisted in a mean way.

"I don't know, Sharon," Susie said. "Why don't we ask your *babushka* what she thinks?"

I raised my eyebrows. Wow, not only was that the most I'd ever heard one of the twins say independently, but I'd learned that Susie was the one who would go for the jugular.

"What's a babushka?" Becca asked.

"It's a Russian grandmother," Jane replied.

"Sharon's Russian?" Becca asked in shock.

"No, not at all!" Sharon said, flustered. Two bright spots of red flamed on her cheeks. "I mean, my grandmother is, but that's because she escaped from there and came to America. She's no communist. She's a real American."

"Well so are we," Susie said.

The team squabbled as everyone dragged Soviet skeletons out of the closet.

Nancy, who was the least interested in the fight eventually broke her silence.

"Isn't it obvious who it is?" She said in a bored voice while she inspected her nails for dirt.

"Not really," I said. For a fleeting instant, Nancy met my eyes. Was she going to accuse me so she could bring me down a notch?

"It's Linda," Nancy said. My first instinct was relief. Then horror kicked in.

"What?" Linda said, sputtering with surprise. She recovered quickly, her shock turning to anger. "Why you little *puta*," she said, moving in on Nancy.

"Hey!" Chris shouted, breaking the girls up just as Linda had grabbed the collar of Nancy's jersey. They glared at each other like prizefighters.

The accusation made no sense. Why would Linda want anyone to outhit her? Her softball career wasn't over after this tournament. It had just begun at the collegiate level. No coach at UCal would have her start after getting blown out of the water in a high-stakes tournament. No way she wanted to lose. Not like this. She would never give up the signs.

"Why don't we all just get showered up and have a team meeting later to talk about this?" Chris suggested.

"I think we should sort this out now," Nancy said crossing her arms. "My uncle would be very interested to learn about what's been happening our her team."

Coach gulped visibly at the mention of Nancy's uncle.

Nancy's great uncle was a State Senator, one who was fiercely anti-communist. He once made a national issue out of the team colors for a Cincinnati middle school. Calling themselves the "Red Devils" was poisoning our country's young minds, he said. Eventually, the outcry was so bad that the school ended up just changing its mascot to a bear and switching to harmless blue and gold. The principal spent weeks explaining that he was in no way a communist sympathizer.

Nancy's family was so proud of the news clippings. Her uncle the Senator said that he was on "high alert" for any Soviet leanings. Anyone caught trying to erode this country's moral fibre would have to answer to him.

The person I was the sorriest for when that happened was the poor principal. It was just a team name, and his job ended up on the line. People were so angry, it was a miracle he didn't get fired. Even waving the red flag of a fabricated communist threat was enough to agitate the bulls of American democracy. And the only thing that ever seemed to appease them was consequences: removals, firings, suspensions.

The same thing was happening to our team. And they were zeroing in on Linda. I thought of Jem, afraid to speak up in case no one would take his side. I needed to defend Linda.

"Linda doesn't have any motive for passing our signs along," I said.

"Sure she does," Nancy said.

"Like what?" I asked, challenging her.

"I can think of a big one," she said, her voice haughty. "Linda has the most to gain from communism."

My jaw dropped from the sheer rudeness of her claim. Mama would have horrors if she knew we were talking about money like this. Sure, Linda's family was poor. We all knew it. But no one dared say it out loud. It just was not done.

I turned to Jane for reassurance. She was the smartest girl on the team and the one we could count on to tell it straight.

"I guess that's true," Jane said quietly. I was crushed.

"And there you have it," Nancy said, throwing her hands up in a 'what more do you want from me gesture.'

Why didn't Jane say something to defend Linda? The disappointment must have shown on my face because Jane spoke up again.

"Just because I said that could be right, doesn't mean I believe Linda did it," she said.

Judging from the tension of the room, the girls didn't buy it. Linda said nothing. She hung her head with resignation. Her mother had once been fired from a housekeeping job after she was accused of stealing an heirloom brooch. It was later found pinned to the collar of a forgotten coat, but Linda's mother was never offered her job back.

Shame flushed my cheeks. It was so easy to blame the outsider when things went wrong. As some of the only Mexicans in town, Linda's family was probably used to misplaced suspicions. Their otherness scared us. They didn't play by Mama and Daddy's rules. And someone who didn't follow the rules was frightening. Which is why when something went wrong, they were the natural choice to place the blame. After all, it couldn't be one of us, could it? Those of us who made sure to go along with everyone else, do everything right, fit in perfectly? Of course not. It had to be one of them.

This logic always made sense to me anytime some random crime ripped through town. A dead body. A break-in. It must be some drifter. Someone unknown to our parts, who didn't know the way things were. The set of rules we had all agreed to. But now that Linda was taking the fall, the sheer unfairness of it sat heavy on my conscience.

I'd had enough of Nancy Bell's witch hunt. Surely, calmer adult heads would prevail.

"Coach? Chris?" I asked. "What do you think?" There was an edge of pleading to my voice. A please, do the right thing here note of despair.

Chris opened her mouth to speak but Coach cut her off.

"Ruiz. You're benched," he said.

Linda let out a little sound that was a mix between a gasp and a sob.

"Coach. Please," she said.

He ignored her and kept talking.

"We're going to use Tessa on the mound next game. I'll make up new signals and let Tessa and Karen know right before the game starts. Be prepared. It'll be sloppy, but we'll make it work."

He walked off briskly. Tears started to slip down Linda's cheeks in earnest now.

"Hit the showers, ladies," Chris barked, breaking up the moment. "My patience with this drama has reached the end. I expect to see you in the common room in two hours to review the tape. It's not going to be pretty."

One by one, the girls drifted off and turned their backs on Linda's despair.

"I didn't do it," Linda said, pleading with us. I was the only one left to hear her.

"I know," I said, stepping forward to put my hand on her shoulder. My heart broke for her.

She held if for a moment and met my eyes with gratitude. It was the most emotion Linda had ever shown, and in a minute it was gone. Her face hardened as her cheeks dried.

"I can't wait to leave this fucking place," she said.

Chapter 26

I stayed in the changeroom long after the other girls had gone. That was it? We just cut our star pitcher without proof? The wrongness of it all weighed heavy in my stomach. I wasn't exactly being selfless. How the hell were we supposed to win without Linda? We needed her. I needed her, really. Because if we didn't win this tournament, I could kiss Arizona goodbye.

I had to find Coach and plead Linda's case. I ran back to the dorms and took the stairs two at a time until I reached his room.

I pounded on the door. No answer. I started to bang again.

Jem came out of the room next to Coach's.

"What are you doing?" He asked.

"Looking for Coach. I need to talk to him," I replied.

I avoided his eyes. After my night with Michael and our morning talk, I couldn't face him straight on. But I didn't have time to sort out my Jem fixation right now. I had bigger fish to fry. My future was at stake.

"About Linda?" Jem asked.

"Yes, about Linda."

Jem came closer and I backed up. I needed to keep my distance, like with the electrical fence they kept around the horses at the stable. If I accidentally touched him, I'd be jolted to my core. I was being a fool, but I couldn't help myself. Something had shifted inside me, and Jem was a danger to the natural order of my life. I needed to avoid him at all costs.

"He's not going to change his mind, you know," he said. His words angered me instantly.

I crossed my arms. "We'll see," I replied and banged on the door again.

The corners of Jem's mouth bent upwards and I tried not to notice how his face was transformed when he smiled.

"Coach isn't there. He said he was going down to the cafeteria for a popsicle," he said.

Oh great. I was going to try to reason with someone who was licking sugar water off a frozen treat.

"Ok, thanks," I said.

I turned to leave and Jem reached to stop me. I froze as electricity ran through my bones and set my heart on fire. Where had this even come from? It was just stupid, sullen Jem. Whatever it was, it was wrong. I shoved the feeling deep into a teeny tiny box inside me, banished to a faraway shelf in the attic of my mind.

"He's not going to change his mind," Jem repeated. "But I think it's important that you try. Blowing off things you think are wrong isn't the way to change things."

He wanted to say more but stopped himself. We weren't just talking about Linda, but him running away from Mr. Fredericks. In the box, in the box, in the box. I willed myself to ignore

Jem's warm hand on my arm. I needed to save Linda's place on the team while there was still time to sway Coach. I needed to undo this mistake and save my own skin in the process.

I found Coach outside the cafeteria struggling with his popsicle wrapper.

"Damn thing," he said as he fumbled with the cellophane. He saw me walking determinedly toward him and sat down on a ratty plaid couch in the hallway with resign.

"I figured I'd be seeing you sooner rather than later. Let me guess. You're here to talk about Ruiz. Am I right? Have a seat."

I hesitated, some of my righteousness deflated with Coach's expectation. I prepared for a fight, but Coach was acting like we were about to have a chit chat outside Church. He broke his popsicle in half and offered me one stick.

"Come on Bennet, your mother told me you like the pink ones. Humor me here."

What a weird thing for Mama to share. But I took the offered half and sat down gingerly. I sunk awkwardly into the old and saggy cushions. I tried to cross my legs in the best deb class style. Mama truly hated women who sat like cowboys. Eventually, I just had to give up and sit with two wide legs apart to stay upright. Undignified. I took a deep breath and began.

"It is about Linda. I don't think it's fair that she got cut. There's no proof that she did anything wrong," I said.

Coach sighed deeply. "I agree with you," he said.

"It's just that we only have Nancy's word and then everyone agreed with her and then it was just like mob mentality and then, wait. What? Did you say that you agree with me?"

He rubbed his bleary eyes.

"Yeah, kid. I said I agree with you. It isn't fair that I cut Linda."

I was confused. "Then why did you?" I asked. My voice went up in an annoying childish way. I needed to get it under control. There was nothing attractive about grown women who whine.

"Because the rest of the team thinks she did it," he said with a shrug. The admission made him sad and old.

"I don't understand," I replied.

Coach was sympathetic.

"I think you understand better than you realize," he said. "Sometimes, it's all about perception. If the team thinks that the problem has been solved, they'll play like winners. If they think their pitcher is a spy, they'll play like shit. Pardon my French."

"That's bullshit!" I said, crossing my arms. "And I'm not excusing anything."

Coach patted my arm and then hoisted himself off the couch like he was struggling out of quicksand.

"Sorry, kid. Sometimes that's just life."

I scowled in response.

"Do me a favor," he said, walking away. "Let's keep that between, us, ok? You need to trust that I know what I'm doing."

I didn't reply. The melted popsicle dripped down my hand. I tried to lick up the mess then chucked the whole thing away in disgust. Coach was right when he said I understood the value of perception. After all, it was what being a debutante was all about. Scratch that, it was what being in Mama and Daddy's world, no, our world, was all about.

Take my own family, for Christ sakes. Moonbeam Kathleen was a single mother traipsing off to God knows where. Mama didn't get out of bed half the time. And if I was being totally honest, Daddy liked the taste of scotch a little too much for polite society. Plus the two of them screaming at each other behind closed doors was something we didn't want the neighbors to find out about.

And yet they were obsessed with presenting me as the perfect little lady at the Cotillion Ball. We'd all put on fancy clothes and pretend that nothing was wrong like a bunch of phoney baloneys. I'd probably be permanently retired from softball by that point, but no one would ever know it from the smile on my face. Why did we even bother? Maybe because it was just easier to go along with whatever everyone thinks is right and ignore the ugly truth underneath. It was simpler to make me into a perfect debutant than to expose the fault lines in our family.

Just like it was easier to believe that Mr. Frederick was a war hero than a racist pig.

Or how I've held on to Michael because it was expected from me instead of admitting what I really wanted.

Why did I avoid looking at the dark places? Was it because I was afraid of my own motivations?

I wasn't going to tell anyone what Coach really thought about Linda. He was right, this would help the team play better. And I desperately needed us to win. We would manage without her.

To help myself, I would turn a blind eye. Rather than find out what was really happening on the team, I would let Coach scapegoat Linda. It was the easiest way.

A heaviness settled on me as I got up to leave. My stomach cramped and it wasn't just from the melted pink popsicle.

Chapter 27

I slept restlessly the night we cut Linda. I had the room to myself now. She had packed her things shortly after getting benched and called her brother to take her home. There wasn't much point in staying here. She wasn't allowed to play, and it was doubtful anyone wanted her around anyway. All Linda had left was two measly words hastily scrawled on a scrap of paper: *good luck.*

I crumpled the note as hard as I could and hurled it in the wastebin. I didn't deserve luck. Not after I had decided to go along with Coach's plan.

Linda would be fine, she still had her scholarship. Coach said he would call OU and make sure they knew that she was still a great player. Chris was handling the media. The official line for Linda's abrupt departure was "family emergency." There was always an easy lie to cover the hard truth.

Sometime after midnight my mind finally calmed enough to drift off to sleep. I was on the edge of dreams when the wail of sirens shattered my calm. I bolted upright in bed. The piercing alarm alternated between loud and louder shrieks. The lights flashed. Was that a fire alarm? I jammed my lumpy pillow over my head, trying to muffle the sound when Jane crashed into my room in her long nightgown, glasses askew.

"Put some shoes on and let's go," she said. "Chris says we're headed down to the fallout site in the basement."

"The what?" I asked as I scrambled behind her.

"The school has a nuclear bunker in the basement of this building. We're going to wait there until we get an all-clear signal," Jane said.

My blood ran cold. Oh God, was Daddy right this whole time? Had it finally happened? Had nuclear war started? I had visions of bombed-out cities and decimated landscapes. Warning films we'd watched in school outlined the horrors of nuclear war. I remembered the drills we'd run through, but there were no desks to hide under in this residence. What else could I do? Shit, I should have paid closer attention in class! Pinpricks of sweat beaded my forehead.

Mama and Daddy. Where would they go if something happened? Would I ever get to see them again? It was easy to dismiss people like Nancy's uncle as paranoid until you realized that there was truly a threat of horrific consequences.

I gripped Jane's hand. "Jane, do you think this is for real?"

She tried to shrug casually, but her eyes were afraid.

"Bigger towns and cities have drills constantly. This could be one of those times," she said.

The rest of the team was in the hallway, eyes bright with fear. Nancy slept in a silk teddy, of course. Becca whimpered and clutched her stuffed bear as we moved to the basement. The stairwell glowed with flashing red lights. We rushed down the stairs until we collided with the Soviet team.

"Where do you think you're going?" Nancy asked Valentina, who was at the head of the group.

"Our coach says we go to the basement," the pitcher replied, eyeing Nancy's frothy lingerie. All the Russians wore matching yellow pyjama tops and bottoms.

"Excuse me, but I don't think so," Nancy said. If your country is attacking us, you get the pleasure of meeting armageddon out in the open."

"Yeah," the twins said, pushing forward.

Valentina swallowed hard. For the first time, I registered an expression on her face. She was scared. Good. If we had to suffer because of her country, she should feel the same amount of terror that we did.

Valentina tried to push past us down the stairs. Nancy blocked her and gave her a little shove.

"*Vziatochnik*," Valentina said, the word coming out like sharp hiss between her teeth. I didn't have to speak Russian to know it wasn't a nice one.

"Say it again in English," Nancy said. "I dare you."

"I do not think you would like it very much if I did," Valentina replied, her eyes narrowed to slits.

More Soviet players gathered around Valentina. I held my breath, waiting for someone to light the fuse. I didn't like Nancy, but I'd have her back in a fight. The siren wailed incessantly.

"Alright ladies, let's break it up," Chris said, hustling down the stairs. "I have it on good authority this is just a drill. The alarm will probably stop as soon as we get to the shelter."

No one moved. Chris grabbed both Nancy and Valentina by their arms.

"I said, move," she said and dragged them down after her. "Where are your coaches anyway? I guess they don't take these drills as seriously as we do."

The pack of girls mutely followed after Chris into the basement level, with Coach bringing up the rear. Where was Jem? My head swivelled backwards, trying to find him in the crowd. The sirens were somewhat muted below ground. Hot rusty pipes clanked above us. Just as we reached the designated safety area, the screeching stopped.

Chris threw up her hands.

"What did I tell you? Just a drill," she said. "I knew it would stop as soon as we got down here. Now back to bed, everyone. We all have practice tomorrow and breakfast is at oh-eight-hundred sharp."

My knees wobbled with relief. I balled my fists to ease my shaking hands. Jane gave me a weak smile.

"I told you it was probably a drill," she said, as rattled as me.

I walked back up to my room on numb legs and tried to settle back into my bunk. But the adrenaline had me vibrating under the covers. There was no way I was sleeping now. I threw my blanket off in disgust. I needed some damn air, and I needed it now.

When I got to the roof, Jem was already there watching the lights on campus.

"Is this where you were the whole time?" I asked, pulling down the hem of my XL Indians shirt. I should have put on some pants. I crossed my arms over my chest.

Jem didn't turn around.

"I thought that if the warning was for real, I'd rather meet my death out in the open than hidden in some grimy basement," he said.

"That's smart," I said.

It had never even crossed my mind to do anything other than what I was told. Jem knew what he wanted and wasn't afraid to choose his own path. Tonight he'd decided to face death straight on rather than huddle in the basement with the rest of us cowards. He was actually brave. Unlike me. I couldn't even be honest about my real feelings. It was too hard and I was too much of a chicken.

Suddenly, I was the one being watched. Jem's steady dark eyes searched my face.

"What?" I asked, self-conscious again. I folded my arms back over myself.

"Coach told me about your offer to Arizona. Thinks you're waffling. You have to take that scholarship, you know that right? You owe it to yourself. To your game," he said.

I examined my feet, suddenly fascinated by the gravel scattered along the ground.

"Well?" Jem prompted.

I met his gaze. "It's probably not going to happen," I admitted.

"Don't say that," he said. "Why not?"

It was too hard to explain. There was no way he would understand the expectations, the path already neatly laid out before me.

"My parents don't think it's a good idea. I couldn't even convince them to fly me out there," I said.

"Then hop on a bus. Or drive," Jem said. "I leave next week. You could hitch a ride with me. We'll road trip it."

He smiled. If only it were that simple.

"It's a little more complicated than that," I said, imagining Mama and Daddy's reaction to the news that I'd taken off with a strange boy they didn't know. A black boy at that.

"No, it can really be that easy," he replied.

His face was so open and honest, I wanted desperately to believe him. Was going to Arizona really as easy as climbing into the passenger seat of a car?

"I'll think about it," I said.

He grabbed both of my hands with his. A charge ran up from my fingertips and down to my very toes. My heart fluttered in my chest. This was the feeling I wasn't allowed to have. But up here on the roof under the moonlight, after I thought we were all going to die, it was harder to fight.

"Do, Bliss. Really think about what you want."

"I will," I said. "I promise."

I couldn't help myself. I reached out to stroke his face, gently running my fingers down his cheek. His skin was hot under my touch. Jem was hardly breathing, like I was a frightened rabbit that might suddenly decide to bolt. What did I want? In that moment, I knew exactly who I wanted.

Slowly, I lifted my face up to his. To reach Jem, I had to get on my tiptoes. He smelled like sunshine and freshly cut grass. Sofly, I pressed my lips to his. I lingered there for a moment, waiting for him to respond. When he didn't, I backed away, flushing bright red.

Oh my God, Bliss. You idiot. You need to go somewhere and die now.

"I, uh, I'm sorry," I said.

Whatever I'd been feeling had only been in my head.

"I shouldn't have done that. Forget it happened," I said.

Mortified, I bolted for the exit. In two long strides, Jem caught up with me. He grabbed my waist and whirled me around, dipped me over and crushed my mouth with his.

My chest was ablaze and the heat spread outwards. My head spun and I melted into his arms as the kiss went on and on. Jem was everywhere, his hands in my hair, his mouth at my neck. I lost track of where he ended and I began. His smell engulfed me as I burned and burned hotter than the hottest Southern hot sauce. The sirens could start roaring again and I wouldn't move from this spot for a second. Every ounce of my being had been created to be touched by Jem's hands.

I'd been kissed lots of times before. I'd even gone all the way. But I had never, felt this way before. It wasn't just lust that was driving me. I felt like my whole body had been split in two and happiness was pouring out of me in rainbow waves. Michael had never made me feel like this.

Michael. Oh Goddammit, Bliss. What the hell was I doing?

Remembering my boyfriend, the one who I should have been kissing, threw cold water on my passion. I wrenched away from Jem, out of breath.

"Bliss," he said, his voice raw. "I've wanted that for so long."

Jem's eyes glittered as brightly as the stars above, his breathing quick. He'd never been more handsome than he was in that moment. Oh, his beautiful face. Jem looked at me like I was a present on Christmas morning. I wanted to throw myself into his muscular arms, to ride away across the country with him and never come back.

But what was I supposed to do? Just kick the perfect boyfriend to the curb? Cut myself off from my family? Turn my back on my whole life? All for one kiss? The most amazing, earth-shattering kiss of my life, yes. But the price for another one was too steep.

Jem pushed the hair out of my eyes.

"Bliss," he said, but I cut him off.

"I can't," I said. "We shouldn't have. I'm sorry."

I turned around quickly, so I wouldn't see his face.

This time when I walked to the exit, he didn't stop me.

Chapter 28

The morning of game three dawned hot and bright. My throat was parched from sleeping hard in a hot room and I picked crust from my eyelashes. I needed water desperately. It was going to be a scorcher. Good. I wanted the weather to match my intensity. Mama and Daddy were coming to see me play, and it was my last chance to prove to them that this was my destiny. Win, and I would be an undisputed hero. To deny me the chance to play at a college level would be nothing short of criminal. Lose, well hell, I didn't want to think about that one yet.

I dressed methodically in my Team USA uniform, making sure each hair ribbon was perfectly in place. I applied my makeup with a precision that would make Mama proud. The face in the mirror was flawless, cold. Perfect. I didn't want to betray any weakness today. We had breakfast with the Soviets and there was no way I'd let them see my puffy morning face. No one could rattle me. Not Jem, not that awful Valentina. I was here for one reason only: to win.

The sound of clinking cutlery and teenage gossip was subdued in the dining hall as girls silently chewed their meals.

"Team meeting, two hours," Chris announced.

I forced oatmeal into my churning stomach and left without a word to anyone. I didn't want to hang around and get caught up in the other girls' nerves. I needed to kill time without going crazy.

Almost in a trance, I walked to the ball diamond. I wanted to stake out the location of my last stand. Flies buzzed in the heat of the day. I shielded my eyes to take in the field and was surprised by the circus atmosphere. Clumps of spectators were already walking in from the full parking lot, dragging coolers and lawn chairs. News vans had pulled right to the edge of the field and were setting up their equipment behind home plate. Vendor tents outside the ball club sold cotton candy, spirit towels, and mini flags. Music from competing boomboxes blasted through the air.

"Feeling nervous?" Asked a nasally British voice behind me.

It was that pushy reporter from the beginning of the tournament, wearing a Yankees cap and a cheap polyester button-up shirt. I'd completely forgotten him in the turbulence of the first two games. But his sweaty red face was another guilty reminder. If we lost today, Northern Lights would be heading home with the Soviets. Poor horsey.

"No," I said, struggling to keep my voice flat and expression calm.

"Cool customer, I like it," he said, undeterred by my terseness. Listen, can you tell me who's pitching for Team USA today?"

I arched my brow. I knew where this was going, and I sure as hell did not want to talk about it. That was in the past. I couldn't dwell on Linda's absence today.

"You can ask Chris Phillips any questions about the lineup. In fact, I'm not supposed to be talking to you at all. You know that," I said.

The reporter brushed me off. "Yeah, yeah, but you aren't here with your team right now either, which means you don't mind going off on your own a little bit. Shame about Linda Ruiz. I'm not sure I buy the rumors about her either. Tell me something, you mad about it, love?"

Was I mad about it? I WAS FURIOUS. I wanted to scream and tear my hair and stamp my feet at the unfairness of it all. That was the thing, wasn't it? Life was unfair. But a good debutante never let the world see her sweat. I channelled Mama's best steel velvet voice. It was the tone she used when dealing with the most unpleasant public situations, like when Daddy had too much to drink at the club and spilled his whiskey down Miss Lockhart's bosom.

"I don't question my coach's decisions," I said.

He didn't need to know that I had done exactly that when Coach cut Linda.

"Is that so? Anyone who did?" He persisted.

"I'd rather we ended our conversation. You're making me uncomfortable," I said. Anyone listening with eyes shut would have sworn it was Mama talking.

"Aw, come on, sweetheart. Give me something to work with here. Those Reds have all kinds of dirt to spill about you," he said and stepped closer to touch my arm.

"Hey fella, take a hike. The lady said she doesn't want to talk."

George stood with his arms crossed over his chest, challenging the reporter to say another word. Peggy hovered next to him, eyebrows raised. They wore matching jean shorts and hand-painted Go USA! shirts.

The reporter put up his hands in mock surrender.

"Take it easy, geezer. I'm just asking a few questions here."

"I think you're done," George said, taking a step forward, his pale face flushed.

Despite being happy to see them, I bit back my annoyance. I was handling the situation. Why would that pesky reporter listen to George when he wouldn't listen to me? With a tip of his cap, the Brit high-tailed it away to pester someone else. I was grateful to see him go.

"Bliss!" Peggy said, running forward to embrace me and my annoyance melted away.

"I didn't know you guys were coming today," I said. I wished she were here in uniform instead of her civvies.

"How could you think we'd miss it?" She asked.

I scuffed the dirt. "I don't know, wedding stuff?"

Peggy laughed. "Don't be silly. There's no way George would let me miss out on this. He's the one who packed up the car and made all the arrangements."

George blushed faintly. "I know how important the team is to her," he said.

"Awww," Peggy said, tilting her head to the side. "What a sweetheart."

George reddened even more and I laughed. So maybe George wasn't the best looking man but he had to be one of the kindest. No, the way he treated Peggy went beyond kindness. What was it? It was respect. Not just for her, but for the things she cared about. It had been Peggy's decision not to play, but George still understood what softball meant to her. What was that kind of relationship like?

If I didn't have softball, I wanted that kind of happiness. Peggy and George made getting married seem not that bad. In fact, they made it seem pretty good. Could that kind of love replace the thrill of swinging the bat and hitting the sweet spot? Or the rush from snagging a tricky throw? Or turning two on a hard grounder? Maybe. From where I was, that kind of love seemed very far away.

"We're not the only ones who came to watch," George said when he recovered, nodded to a familiar figure making his way toward us.

Michael. My heart curled and contracted with guilt. I thought he couldn't come because of work. Could he tell I had kissed someone else by my face? Heat spread across my cheeks.

"Hey sexy," he said, bending down to kiss me.

He'd dressed for the heat, in a navy polo terry shirt and matching shorts, but no hat. He didn't like to mess his hair.

"Hi," I said. "I didn't know I'd see you today. Peggy and George told me you were coming."

He smiled a feline grin. "Did I surprise you? Groovy. I'm here with your folks. We couldn't miss our girl's last softball game."

My smile faltered. My last game. Maybe. I could still turn it around. I could prove to Mama and Daddy and even Michael this is what I was meant to do.

Michael was oblivious to my discomfort, pleased with something. He led me by the hand over to a set of bleachers and indicated for me to sit. He stayed on his feet.

"I wanted to get you something today," he said, pulling a velvet ring box out of his pocket. "You know, to mark an ending and celebrate new beginnings."

Oh God, no. I hoped to hell this wasn't actually happening. I fought every instinct to bolt. I wasn't ready for this yet. To my somewhat relief, Michael didn't get down on his knee. Instead, he made a dramatic show of opening the box. Inside was a delicate gold ring with an emerald the size of a Chiclet. It sparkled in the light.

"To match your gorgeous eyes," he said.

"I... thank you," I managed to sputter out. What did it mean?

"It's for your right hand," Michael said. "It's a promise ring. Bliss, we don't have to get married until you're finished at Bryn Mawr. We don't even have to get engaged yet, but I want to make my intentions clear. I promise that one day I will swap this out for a diamond ring bigger than your mother's."

A promise ring. It was more than a promise to be married one day. It was a marker. It told the world I was taken. I belonged to Michael.

"Try it on," he said. "Your mom helped me get the size."

Mama. Of course. She'd be pleased as punch about this. Daddy too. He was probably already planning the business merger to go along with the family merger. As a Bennet-King, I'd make for one hell of a new steel dynasty.

Michael reached out to slip the ring on. I tore my hand away, sure the ring would burn me, would cut off my circulation and make my throwing hand useless. The emerald clattered into the dirt.

"Bliss, what the hell?" Michael said, his mouth twisted in anger.

Could I take this ring from him? After what I'd done? When I knew what I really wanted?

Refusing would mean it was over. I wasn't that crazy.

Michael was the perfect boyfriend, the perfect man. He had done everything perfectly. This should be every girl's dream. Just because I wasn't as delighted as I should be at this moment, didn't mean it wasn't right. This is what nice girls did. This was my reward after letting him take my virginity. You heard stories about girls, whose boyfriends said things, made promises to get what they wanted and then broke them all, shrugged them off and left those girls with nothing but a ruined reputation. Michael wasn't like that. I was so lucky to have him. I couldn't ask for a better boyfriend, fiance, or future husband.

I scooped down to pick the ring up, giggling to cover my swirl of emotions. It was just a ring. It didn't have power over me. It couldn't hurt me. But I still couldn't put it on.

"Oops, I'm so clumsy," I said. "Michael, this ring is beyond perfect, but I'm afraid I'll ruin it if I wear it out there today."

Frustration flashed across his face, but I soothed him quickly, undoing the clasp on my necklace. I strung the ring on the chain, and it swooped down, clattering against the gold locket Mama and Daddy had given me for my sixteenth birthday. I tucked the chain back under my uniform. Out of sight, out of mind.

I touched Michael's hand to my chest. "Right next to my heart," I said.

"Aren't you a sweetheart?" He said and pulled me close for a kiss.

He was such a good kisser. It was nice. So what if my chest didn't burn the way it had when Jem kissed me? Mama always warned me that if I played with fire, I'd get burned. Safe, dependable Michael was better.

Michael pulled away and patted my head. "Alright, babe. I'll let you get to it. After, I'll drive you home. Sound good?"

I nodded mutely and Michael sauntered off. I barely heard his parting words, transfixed by the person watching us from the dugout.

Jem sat motionless on the players' bench, staring at Michael's retreating back.

Chapter 29

A hot wave of shame washed over me. How much had Jem seen? I needed to explain that I hadn't actually put Michael's ring on.

"Jem," I called, jogging over to him.

Jem stood up and stepped into the sunlight. His lips were pressed together so tightly, his mouth formed a thin white line like a softball stitch. His eyes were flat like skipping stones at the bottom of the lake. But it was the blankness of his face that frightened me the most. I didn't need to ask. He had seen everything.

"I need to talk to you," he said, his voice hard like he was trying to keep it under control.

"Okay," I said, crossing my arms defensively across my chest.

I knew where this was going, and I wasn't ready to talk about me and Michael. Or what had happened between me and Jem. The memory of his touch flashed involuntarily through my mind, sending a shiver up my spine. This was not the day to get caught up in this.

"What just happened between you two over there? I saw him give you something," Jem asked.

Anger bloomed hot and tight across my chest. Who did Jem think he was?

"How is that any of your damn business?" I asked.

Jem's mouth twisted. "You deserve more than him," he said.

The laugh slipped out before I could control myself. Only Jem would say that. It was obvious to any sane person on earth that Michael was a total catch.

"I'm being serious, Bliss," he said, grabbing my arm. His grip was too tight. I shook him off.

"You need someone who excites you and encourages you, not someone who tries to cram you into a mold of what he wants you to be. Some stupid little debutante. Can't you see you're so much more than?"

I stepped away, cradling my arm. How dare he tell me who I was, what my life was about? Did he think that because he kissed me once, he knew me? He didn't know me. Or my family. He wasn't from my world. He didn't know what the right thing to do was. What was expected. Or the consequences of not doing those things.

When I spoke, I couldn't control the tremble in my voice.

"What do you know about it anyway?" I demanded.

Jem's chin jutted out stubbornly.

"I know what I see," he said. He paused.

"I know what I feel," he continued, in a softer voice.

"You don't know anything. Michael is perfect. He's good-looking. He's handsome. He goes to Princeton. He's charming. His family is wealthy," I said. I listed off his stats on my fingers, checking off a boyfriend list. "He drives a nice car. He can order off a menu in French. He's got great hair. My father likes him. Umm..."

I had run out of reasons.

"You forgot something," Jem said, a pained smile teasing the corner of his lips. He shook his head.

"What's that?"

"Do you love him?"

The question blindsided me. Did I love Michael? I probably should. Jem had exposed me, but I wasn't about to give him the satisfaction of being right.

"What does that have anything to do with it? You said that Michael wasn't good enough, and I just gave you a list of reasons why he was."

In one quick motion, Jem covered the space between us until we were inches apart. He leaned down as if he was going to kiss me. My heart raced in anticipation. I'd shoved every feeling I'd had for Jem down deep inside me until it was a dam, ready to burst. If he touched me now, I was afraid of what destruction would come from the overflow. I braced for the feel of his lips, closing my eyes.

Instead, his breath tickled my neck as he whispered in my ear.

"Who are you trying to convince that you should be with Michael?" He asked. "Me? Or you?"

My eyes flew open. Humiliation twisted my stomach and colored my cheeks. Jem had peeled off my mask and seen the Bliss hiding underneath. She was an ugly, cowardly girl and I resented the hell out of Jem for dragging her into the open. For forcing me to awknowledge at her. There was a reason why I kept her hidden away. Why I took Mama's advice and only showed my sparking deb self. I didn't like the hidden me.

Hot rage bubbled over. Goddamn him. I drew back my hand and slapped Jem across the face. Hard. Jesus. Was I the kind of girl who hit people now? I was out of control.

Jem said nothing. He didn't even touch the stinging spot on his cheek. We glared at each other, the sound of violence in the air.

When I couldn't take it anymore, I ran away, into the locker room.

Goddamn him for rattling me. On today of all days.

And goddamn me for caring. Goddamn it all.

Chapter 30

I sat in the locker room in a daze. Nervous chatter swirled around me, but I concentrated on tying and retying my cleats. Over and over again I pulled the laces, trying to get the ideal tightness that was firm yet flexible. I couldn't get it right.

I tugged until the soft cotton of my laces left red welts on my palms. Not good. I needed soft hands for the game. I rubbed the sweat from my palms onto my shorts.

Chris was talking. Some last-minute instructions about the style of play she wanted to see today. I didn't hear a word. I could guess what she wanted. She needed to bring a win back for Softball USA.

For the first time, it struck me that her fate was also riding on the outcome of this game. I hoped I could bring home that W for her. Both our futures were riding on it.

Instead of listening, I was distracted by Coach standing with Karen and Tessa in the corner of the room. They were working through their last-minute signals. I shook my head. It was bull-shit, and Coach knew it.

The way Linda was treated was deeply unfair. But that was life, wasn't it? Deeply, horribly unfair. It wasn't fair that I'd had every opportunity in the world, but wanted to throw it all away. Linda had been given nothing but was fighting to have it all. Softball was a way for her to get the things I had grown up with as my right. I was selfish, unworthy of the advantages my parents had provided.

This game was it. Win, and I'd keep fighting to play. Lose, and I'd accept it was over. I'd be happy with what I had, the way I should have been the entire time. I would be a smiling, happy debutante for Mama. I'd respect The Popps. I would pledge myself to Michael. I would forget all the doubts. I would drown that tiny, greedy voice in my head that always wanted more.

Coach came forward and said a few words about victory. I closed my eyes and visualized my swing. I imagined myself cracking the ball so hard it flew over the center-field fence. In my mind, I rounded the bases grinning, the sun shining in my face.

Coach clapped his hands together and the speech was over. I grabbed my glove and followed the other girls to the glowing exit. Outside, my future waited.

Chapter 31

Top of the seventh and we still hadn't managed to catch a break. The good news was neither had the Russians, and the score was tied 0-0.

I tried to ignore the sweat dripping down my back, running in a hot line down my chest. I wiped my hands for the millionth time. My shorts were damp from my sticky palms.

Even the crowd had started to lose its steam, wilting under the blazing sun and the lack of action. The cheers were getting sporadic and muffled. Kids were getting cranky and one baby wailed. Sure, there'd been a few hits. But only a few and the defence on both sides had been insane. At this rate, we'd be into extra innings for sure. It would take a monster shot to get anyone home. To Tessa's credit, she'd been holding her own all game. Her body was tinier and more compact than Linda's, but she could still bring the heat. She was slowing down though.

There were two out when a Soviet girl with a long, red ponytail got up to bat. Just one more. We needed one more out to leave the top of the inning and get a shot at winning the game. I tensed for the hit. Three pitches went by, and nothing. Two strikes and a ball. We had her.

Tessa wound up, threw, and smack, a laser down the third base line. The ball whizzed by Susie's right ear. She couldn't get her glove over fast enough to catch it. Damn. Nancy scooped the ball up easily in left and threw it to Cher at second base. The runner held at first. That was fine. We were still in it.

"Good stop there, Nancy!" I called out, beating the back of my glove with my right hand. Dust flew up at my touch. "Let's get them with this next one."

Nancy adjusted her ponytail and nodded at me. Whatever I might think of her off the field, we were sisters on the diamond.

Katarina was up next. Pining for the boy back home hadn't done anything to slow down her game. She'd been one of the best hitters of the tournament. She walked to the plate slowly, adjusting her batting gloves and helmet.

Come on, Tessa. Let's do this. Strike her out. Please please, please.

Karen flashed a signal that Tessa shook off. She tried another that Tessa still wasn't happy with. What the hell was going on? Now wasn't the time to start cracking up. Finally, they agreed on a throw.

Tessa wound up, delivered, and... swing and a miss. Katarina's bat whipped around into air. She was here to hit.

The next pitch curved in for a strike.

"That's two!" The twins said.

Two down, one to go. We were nearly there. I reminded myself to breathe and huffed out a loud sigh. I was wound tight, ready to spring into action at the first contact.

Tessa and Karen were disagreeing on the throw again, with Karen insistently calling one pitch, and Tessa shaking her off, confused. Worry wormed through me. No, no, no. She needed to do what Karen said. Karen knew how to call a game. Coach gave the orders, but Karen ran the team from behind home plate. The crowd was restless.

Finally, they settled on a throw. I couldn't see Karen's face behind her mask, but from the way she slammed herself back into position, I could tell she was unhappy. Tessa's shoulders were rigid. She heaved a deep breath and held the ball for an extra second. Finally, she wound up and delivered.

Crack! Katarina hit it hard and long. It soared into center field and the redhead on first took off, tearing through the bases. The ball bounced once before Jane picked it up, just missing the catch out. Dammit. The red head's cleats slapped loud at home base. The Soviets cheered. They had scored what could be the winning point in the last inning.

Blood roared in my ears and I commanded myself to stay calm. Getting worked up wouldn't do us any good. Tessa paced on the mound, getting the last one out of her head.

"Let's go! One more out!" Karen yelled, her voice muffled by the catcher's mask.

Tessa nodded. She was ready. This time there was no confusion about signals.

The Soviet on first took a few steps off the base, bouncing on her feet.

Tessa windmilled in a perfect fastball. The batter swung and connected.

It happened instantly. The runner was off. The ball rocketed my way. Hard grounder. I sprinted toward it, and in one fluid motion, barehanded the ball and slung it to Deb. She was positioned with the foot on the base, arm stretched out as far as possible. The batter was coming, but my throw was faster.

The ball slapped into Deb's mitt seconds before the girl reached first.

"You're out!"

"Yes!" I whooped.

I ran out to Deb and hoisted her up to spin her around. I vowed to never confuse her with her sister again.

I trotted back to the dugout, smile wide on my face.

"What are you grinning about?" Jem snapped. "We're still down by one."

Instantly, my smile dissolved. Asshole. But he was right. I pursed my lips. Regret flashed across his face. He wanted to say something but I didn't give him the chance. I moved to the far side of the dugout.

Coach, as usual, took the softer approach.

"Alright, kids. Bad luck with that last one, but you couldn't keep the tap off forever. Bliss, great stop out there. That's the kind of heads up play I'm talking about. Just phenomenal," Coach said, clapping his hands together. "Now you know what? I'm not even worried about the score. Because we've got a whole inning to get our bats fired up and knock a couple in. Think you can do that?"

"Yeah!" We replied.

Coach cupped his ear, his eyes sparkling. "What's that? I couldn't hear you."

"Yeah!" We screamed.

"That's better," he said. Coach grabbed the batting list and read out the order. "D. Mara! S. Mara! Porter! Bennet! You're up! Let's go."

Karen handed out the Double Bubble. I sat on the edge of the bench and chewed silently, watching the game. Jem's large frame loomed in the entranceway. My body hummed at his proximity but I ignored the feeling. Focus. I just needed to focus.

Deb managed to get on base. She just needed someone to knock her in and we'd be tied.

I closed my eyes and imagined walking up to the plate, getting the perfect pitch and skying the ball over the left fielder's head. Walk-off homer. I'd loop the bases at a relaxed pace, stopping to blow a kiss at Valentina as I touched home.

"Bennet! You're on deck."

I walked out to the warm-up circle and breathed deeply, practising my swing. Becca struck out and we had two down.

Realizing this could be it, the crowd had rallied. "USA! USA!" They chanted, feet stomping and shaking the bleachers. News crews scrambled with their cameras, ready to film the ending of the game. Peggy and George were on their feet screaming my name. I scanned the stands for my parents. They were nearby entranced by something Michael was telling them. They didn't seem to realize I was up to bat. They would when I hit the winning run.

"Up next for Team USA... number 3, Bliss Bennet!" The announcer's voice crackled over the loudspeaker.

I breathed out and counted to 10. This was it. I took my place at home plate.

Valentina smiled slightly at me over the edge of her glove and nodded. It was on. No teasing, no taunting. We were both in the zone. Everyone else fell away. The entire game would be settled between me and her now.

She wound up and her first pitch screamed in. Fast, but low and outside. I didn't flinch. Ball one.

Her face was expressionless.

A pause while the catcher threw the ball back and she readjusted her grip. Valentina hurled the ball again. This time it was high. I stayed stone still.

"Ball two!" The umpire muttered.

I inclined my head to Valentina. Come on. I'm not taking your junk. Give me something I can hit.

The next one across the plate was a fastball. I brought my bat around hard, a second too late. It pinged off the end and went high and foul, popping up and landing near the concession stand.

Damn. I stepped away from the plate and swivelled my core back and forth, trying to reset my form. I found Coach in the dugout and he smiled.

"You got this, kid!" He called over.

Jem was standing next to him, and for a blazing moment, he held my eyes. HIs intensity had nothing to do with us. It was for the game. It was for my ability and his confidence in it. I burned with purpose. Focus. Focus. Breathe. I could do this.

Valentina, ball in hand, took her time readjusting on the mound. She nodded at the pitch call and set for the next throw.

It was fast and low and I chased it to the edge of the plate, pinging it foul again.

Dammit, Bliss. Calm down. That could have been a ball. I'm not giving her this out. She needs to work for it.

I readjusted and waited for the next pitch. Down and low again. Fool me once... I wasn't biting.

"Good eye!" Peggy screamed from the stands.

Full count. This was it. One more pitch to decide the game.

The crowd noise fell away. All I heard was the blood roaring in my ears and my own heart-beat. The edges of my vision blurred out of focus. I could only see one person. Valentina on the mound, the only person in the world who mattered.

She set and relaxed. She'd already decided what to do. Would she try to get me to chase junk? That seemed like a risky move, considering I was on high alert for garbage and not afraid to watch a pitch. Or would she try to put a strike in there? She might think I would play it cautious and watch it go in.

Valentina focused. She was going to throw something I could hit. She wanted me to strike-out looking.

I watched her carefully and time seemed to slow. In a swift motion, she set, windmilled, and released hard. The ball flew straight and true toward me.

My swing was flawless. Elbow up, left foot leading, hips twisting in perfect motion.

I swung for the fence.

And came up with air.

The ball dropped into the catcher's glove seconds after I brought my bat around.

"Strike three, you're out of there!"

Cold panic made me dizzy. My vision blurred. I couldn't believe it.

Valentina had struck me out with the off-speed. I'd fallen for it like a fool.

It was over.

I had just lost the game, the whole tournament, and my future.

Chapter 32

The ringing in my ears wouldn't stop.

I couldn't hear anything. Not the noise from the crowd, not Coach's words of comfort in his post-game debrief. I didn't hear the good sportsman-like three cheers we gave the Soviets. Or whatever Valentina said to me as we went down the line, shaking hands with our opponents.

The piercing wail in my head continued, like the emergency broadcast system on loop. Was I going crazy? I must have been, to think my scheme was going to work. I turned back to the dugout and my knees buckled.

Jane, who had been walking behind me, rushed to steady me.

"You okay?" She asked. I think that's what she asked. Her words and the movement of her mouth weren't connected.

"You need water. We all do. You're dehydrated," Jane said.

She thrust her water bottle in my hands and watched me with sharp eyes until I'd taken a long drink. It tasted like stale rainwater and I fought back the urge to gag it all up.

I caught sight of Mama in the stands and remembered myself. This is what my deb training was for. I would put this embarrassment far, far, behind me and never think of it again. And I would start now. Even if it killed me, I would trick everyone into thinking that everything was fine, everything was normal. Including myself.

The first step, stop acting like something was wrong. With measured movements, I returned Jane's water bottle. Now, smile. I spread my lips into the closest approximation of a grin I could manage, showing my teeth in a hideous grimace.

I pictured my strikeout. I wanted to hurl all over again. No! I would push those thoughts away. Banish them to a place I would never visit.

I needed to straighten up. Walk unhurriedly. Put one foot in front of the other. I was fine, I was fine, I was fine, I was fine. I clenched my fists once and relaxed my hands. I was fine, I was fine, I was fine. Fine, fine, fine. I was fine. I. Was. Fine.

My bottom lip trembled, a sure sign of impending tears. For the love of God, not out here. Not where everyone could see me. Not where Valentina could know that she had truly beaten me. Or where Jem could tell just how crushed I was. If I saw my own pain reflected in his face, I wouldn't make it to the change room with any of my dignity intact.

I bargained with myself. If I could just hold it together until I got to the showers, I would let myself fall apart when I was alone. I could scream and cry and tear my hair and gnash my teeth. But it had to be in private. Not here where people could see me.

"Tough loss out there, ladies," Chris said. "Shower up and see your families."

The twins said something to me and I pretended to hear them. I'd already forgotten my pledge to tell them apart. I calmly stripped out of my uniform, throwing it in a heap on the floor. I left my cleats for good measure. I wouldn't need them ever again.

I wrapped myself in a towel and walked to the shower. So close now. At the end of the row, the fake pleasantness fell off my face. It dropped into the heavy frown I had used so much energy to conceal.

Stupid, Bliss. So stupid. You thought you could be the big hero and save the tournament and yourself. That your insane plot to defy your parents' wishes and move out west for softball would actually work. You're an idiot. An idiot and a terrible softball player. It was all just the stupid dream of a naive fool.

The tears came. I lost track of time sobbing in the shower. My fingers turned into tiny raisins as I cried myself hoarse.

The change room was empty when I emerged. I put on a peppy romper and blow-dried my hair, letting it hang long and loose. I was fastidious with my makeup, primping to glossy perfection. The Cotillion Ball was next week and I would make my debut and go back to my proper place in the world.

I took Michael's promise ring off the chain. I sat on the hard bench in the change room turning it over in my fingers for a long time.

When I stepped into the sunlight, Mama and Daddy, Michael, Peggy and George, were all waiting for me.

I smiled. It was the bright, carefree smile of a happy teenage girl who was sure of her place in the world.

Michael's emerald ring glinted on my finger.

Chapter 33

The days leading up to the Cotillion Ball passed by in grey sludge. I tried my hardest to focus my efforts on the tasks at hand, to find whatever pleasure there was in debutante class.

The Popps perfected our dance steps. When she was through with us, even Bobby Rice had a passable waltz. After he managed to get through an entire dance without stepping on his partner's feet, the old bird wiped away a tear and tried to pass it off as allergies.

For our deb class's community service project, we had pledged to turn an overgrown lot into a playground for the neighborhood children. We hauled, raked, dug, clean, cleared, installed, primed and painted over the week. On workdays, I'd be the first to show up and the last to leave. Sleep only came easy when I was worn out from working. Rosa would run a warm bath for me and I'd soak my sore muscles until I was ready to pass out.

Mama was in constant terror that I would neglect to completely shield every inch of my skin from the sun and end up with freckles before the ball. On days she was feeling up to it, she'd drive by the lot with refreshments for the girls.

"Your mother is always so glamorous," Peggy breathed after Mama showed up in a long pleated white skirt and white silk blouse, an Hermés scarf knottily jauntily around her neck.

"Bliss, darling," Mama said. "The brim on your hat is simply not wide enough. Here, take mine. I want you to cover up your shoulders too."

"Girls look good with a tan, Mrs. Bennet," Nancy said, reeking of the coconut oil she slathered on every day to catch the sun's rays.

Mama disagreed in her well-manned way. "Well, Nancy, that's nice for some. But Bliss's skin is one of her loveliest features. And she doesn't brown up as nice as some of you girls. She just burns."

I smiled tightly. Sometimes Mama talked about me like I was one of her childhood prize ponies. I stood still while she fussed over me. Finally, she'd had enough.

"Well, I should be off," Mama said. "Bliss, do not stay here late by yourself again, there are some unsavory types in the neighborhood."

I colored at Mama's words as she sashayed back down to the car. "Unsavory types" in Mama's language meant Mexicans. Linda's family lived just down the street. I hoped to see her every day, but she never came by. I wanted to knock on her door, but I was so chicken I only got as far as the end of her walk. What would I say? Sorry everyone in this town is awful and says your family should be deported? I'm sure that would go over just peachy.

I looked down the street toward Linda's house. Nancy came and stood beside me. Despite all the manual labor we were supposed to be doing, she managed to stay pristine. It was easy to keep your hair tidy when you didn't actually lift a finger to help.

"I still think I should have called my uncle about her," she said, crossing her arms.

"Mama thinks she's been through enough," I said.

When we got back from Cleveland, there was an article in the paper about the tournament, blaming the loss on Communist interference. Linda wasn't named but in a small town, it was pretty easy to figure out who the reporter meant. Linda's mom nearly lost her job until Mama told all the ladies at the club that it all sounded like a bunch of nonsense to her.

"That's what Coach said, too," Nancy said. She walked away, a cruel smile playing on her lips. "But I guess she's always on Coach's side, isn't she?"

What the hell was that supposed to mean? If Mama were on Coach's side, I'd be getting ready to go to Arizona instead of picking trash out of this abandoned lot. Well, I'd still probably be picking trash out this abandoned lot. But I'd be a lot more excited about it if I were just days away from leaving Elmhurst behind forever.

Oh, to hell with Nancy. I needed to go see how Linda was doing. I at least owed her an apology for blowing the tournament.

Instead of cowering on the walk I strode right to the front door. The house was painted a cheery yellow color and the door was a soft blue. I rang the bell and heard yelling and footsteps.

Linda answered, wearing bellbottoms and a tee, her hair wet from the shower. Her face was stone.

"What do you want?" She asked.

Suddenly, I wasn't so sure coming was the right idea.

"I just, uh—" I said.

"Linda!" Her mother called from inside. "*Quién es?*"

"No one, mami! Just a girl from softball," Linda yelled back.

There was shuffling in the hall and cheerful, plump woman with streaks of white in her dark bun came to the door. She wore a ruffled blue apron and was likely responsible for the tasty cooking smell wafting my way. She smiled at me.

"Come, come," Mrs. Ruiz said in her heavy accent, leading me into the living room, past a large gold crucifix and a framed portrait of the Pope.

The room was about the size of my bedroom. The walls were painted bright green and covered in family photos. Mismatched colored furniture and lush houseplants filled every inch of space. Tucked away in a corner was a tiny alter. Candles were lit around a statue of the Virgin Mary, a picture of Linda, and a softball. Linda followed my gaze.

"I wasn't lying when I said her prayers were in overdrive," she said.

We sat down awkwardly across from each other. Linda's mother bustled into the kitchen.

"I get you something to eat," she said.

"No, Mami!" Linda yelled after her. "She's not staying," she finished, cold eyes on me.

I licked my lips nervously. Linda leaned back into the overstuffed couch and crossed her arms, waiting for me to speak. My words came out in a rush.

"I just came to apologize again about what happened at the tournament. I tried talking to Coach again, but it was too late. I should have done a better job standing up for you. And I wanted to tell you I'm sorry that we lost. I struck out on the last at-bat of the game. I'm sorry that after all that I couldn't even get you a win," I said in one breath.

Linda's face didn't change. "You know what? That shit's in my rearview mirror. I'm done with this place and I don't care anymore," she said, shrugging. "Is that all?"

"I just wanted to wish you luck in Oklahoma. I'm jealous that you're going to keep playing," I said. "I'm done. My career is over."

Against my will, tears formed at the corners of my eyes and threatened to spill over. Linda softened. She hated crying.

"Hey, *suficiente*. That's enough of that," she said, offering me a tissue. "What's the problem? Can't you just keep playing in college?"

"My parents won't let me. I have to go to Bryn Mawr," I said.

Linda sucked her teeth. "Oh, how terrible for you," she said sarcastically. "It must be really difficult to have to go to a fancy school."

I blushed, suddenly ashamed of myself. "I'm sorry," I said again.

Linda waved me off.

"You could just go to Arizona, you know," she said.

I shook my head. "It would be impossible without my parents' support. I can't do it alone," I admitted. "Do you think I'm a coward?"

I stared hard at my feet, afraid to meet Linda's eye.

"No, I think you're lucky," Linda said. "I play softball because I'm good at it. Do I love pitching? Not really. But I do love that I'm going to be the first in my family to go to college. I'm going to get me a good education and a good job and then one day Moms will be able to put her feet up and I'll pay someone to clean her house. It's not going to be easy though. Maybe my kids will have it easy. That's the dream."

And I was just a silly girl who wanted to throw that dream away.

"*A comer!*" Mrs. Ruiz yelled from the kitchen.

"You want to stay for dinner?" Linda asked. "Moms made enchiladas."

I didn't know what those were, but they sure did smell good.

"Tempting," I said. "But I should get home."

Linda walked me to the door and gave me a quick hug.

"You'll be fine, Bennet," she said.

I wanted desperately to believe her.

Chapter 34

The night before the Cotillion Ball, we had Michael over for dinner. Ever since I'd slipped on that promise ring, Mama and Daddy had insisted on spending more time with him. Daddy wanted to get to know his future son-in-law better, he'd say half-threateningly, half-jokingly.

That night, the dining room table had been set with candles and roses. Rosa had tried out a new chicken a l'orange recipe Mama had found in *Good Housekeeping*. Mama never actually did any housework herself, but she made sure to keep on top of all the latest trends.

"It's all part of good household management, Bliss," she'd told me. "Don't worry, we'll have plenty of time to go over all of these things before you need to use them."

She'd smiled at me then, but it didn't reach her eyes. I didn't give a damn about household management. Jem had called the house for me yesterday. Rosa had taken the message, thank God. Jem wanted to know if I still needed a ride. My heart had leapt at the sound of his name. He must have forgiven me for how I'd treated him. But would he forgive me when I told him I couldn't go? I couldn't figure out how to tell him.

Instead, I concentrated on the task at hand. Being a little princess for my parents, the ideal debutante and flawless girlfriend. That night, I'd worn a cream-colored halter jumpsuit. The silky material set off my auburn hair, Mama said. I had it pinned into a low chignon. My only accessories were gold hoops and Michael's ring, of course.

I twisted it around and around as Daddy's poured himself a scotch.

"Just one, I hope, Chip," Mama said anxiously. "There will be wine with dinner."

Daddy slopped an extra-large serving into his cut-glass tumbler.

"I'll have as much as I damn well please, Marie," he said, snatching the glass off the tray.

Mama sniffed and retreated. I said nothing. Relations between the two of them were even more strained than usual these days. Kathleen must have been in touch again, asking for money. Damn her if she had. She'd let me down when I needed her the most.

Daddy took two big gulps of the drink. His eyes challenged me to say something. I didn't.

The doorbell rang.

"Oh, he's here!" Mama said, fluttering around. "Rosa, we need to light those candles! And put the nut trays out! You forgot the nut trays."

Mama was being insane about Michael's visit. The worse things got between her and Daddy, the more she wanted everything to be perfect between me and Michael.

"I'll get it," I said and slowly sauntered to the door. I was dreading this evening.

Michael smiled when I let him in. He wore a plain suit, no tie, with his wide collar spread open to reveal tan skin. He held two bouquets.

"Oh Michael, you shouldn't have," Mama said.

She cooed and fussed over the flowers while Michael took a seat on the couch. He accepted a drink from Daddy and the two of them talked business. That was my cue to tune out.

While they bonded, I fretted over Jem. I should just call. That was the right thing to do, wasn't it? No, I needed to tell him to his face that I wasn't coming. To explain myself.

"Well, now that you're talking mixing business and pleasure, aren't we all just glad Bliss has put this softball nonsense behind her now? It's so hard on the nails!" Mama chirped from the divan, her third glass of wine in hand.

Daddy shot her a dark look. Michael patted my hand. I tried to swallow down the anger that rose up in my throat.

"I'm just happy to have her all to myself now. Before she goes to college in the fall, that is," he said.

Mama waved her hand. "Oh yes, well, she's not necessarily going away for the whole four years," she said, winking at me.

Right. Because I was doing to drop out to get my MRS and become a Stepford Wife. I clenched my fist, leaving red crescent moon nail marks in my palm.

Michael and Daddy laughed and went back to whatever they were talking about. They spent the whole meal in intense discussion while Mama tried and failed to bring the conversation around to something we could all talk about. My mind wandered as they threw around words like, "consolidation," "merger," and "growing the family business." I may as well have been invisible for all the attention either one paid to me.

When the meal was over, Michael sat back, full and happy. He beamed at me.

"Well, Mr. and Mrs. B. I should scoot. Thanks for the groovy meal," he said.

I walked him to the door. He gripped my hand firmly.

"You know," I said, lightly. "Sometimes I get the feeling that you're more excited about spending time with Daddy than you are with me."

Michael laughed. "Oh, Bliss. We're just making sure we can take care of our women," he replied. "You know that you're the one that matters to me."

He leaned down to kiss me as if to prove his sincerity but I ducked out from under him. I pushed the point. I needed to see my choice through clear eyes. If this was going to be my life, I needed to know exactly what I was getting into. My heart pounded in my ears as I searched his eyes with mine.

"Do you really love me? Or is this relationship the easy way into a business merger?" I asked. I held my breath for an answer.

Michael let out a short, surprised bark of laughter.

"Bliss, you know it's nothing like that. I love you," he said.

He leaned down to kiss me once more and I let him. But he never met my eyes.

Chapter 35

If I had to sit underneath the goddamn hairdryer for one more minute I was going to scream. I was trapped in the heat of the cap while the tight curlers stung my scalp.

"Stop squirming," Cher said, holding my legs still. "You're going to mess up the set and then your hair won't be perfect for tonight."

Peggy sat calmly beside me, flipping through a bridal magazine.

"Doesn't this bother you?" I asked.

She shrugged.

"It's best not to think about it and just submit to the dryer. It goes faster that way."

I tapped my nails on the armrest, tugged the hems of my cutoff shorts, and played drums with my rubber soles.

"Okay!" Cher finally said. "You're done! How is it that you're able to sit stock still through the entirety of one of Coach's boring lectures, but you can't spend 30 minutes under the hairdryer?" She asked as I sprung from my seat.

"Coach is interesting," I replied. I was going to have to start bringing a book to salon appointments.

"Well, come here and let me comb you out."

I followed Cher to her station where she had taped up a photo of Donny Osmond along with other fashion magazine clippings. She was spending the rest of the summer working at her mother's salon before starting beauty school in September.

"Isn't he handsome?" Cher asked, blowing the picture a kiss. "He's nearly as good-looking as Jem, don't you think?" She winked at me.

"Jem? Handsome? I wouldn't know. I have a boyfriend," I said and then turned pink. There's no way she could know what happened between us, could she? I shifted uncomfortably in my seat.

Cher grinned wickedly.

"It's okay to look, you know. Anyway, he doesn't give anyone the time of day, does he?"

"No," I said, trying to keep my voice light. "He doesn't."

Jem. I'd finally gotten up the nerve to call him, but his mom told me he was at his part-time job, serving at the club. He left the next day and I was out of chances to talk to him. Unless he was at the ball tonight. I didn't know how I would pin him down to explain myself, but I had to try.

The door to the salon tinkled. Cher smiled.

"Speak of the devil," she said.

I froze. Jem was here? I wasn't ready to face him in person!

"Hi Michael," she said, giving him her sweetest smile. She waggled her eyebrows at me and sashayed away.

Relief and disappointment washed over me in equal measures.

"Michael," I said. "What are you doing here?"

He had a small wrapped package tucked under his arm. He seemed tense.

"Bliss, can I talk to you for a second?"

"Sure," I replied, puzzled.

He led me out into the sunshine. Briefly, panic shot through me. Was he cancelling as my date for tonight? Mama would be furious. Daddy would have to escort me and I'd be humiliated. Color rose to my cheeks. Oh, I'd kill him for this if Mama didn't beat me to it.

"Bliss, I am so sorry about the other night at your house."

Ohhh, he was here to apologize. I relaxed, the tension rolling off my shoulders.

He continued. "I'm not going to lie, I do consider myself very lucky that your Father is who he is, and his interests align with my family's interests. I'm not going to apologize for that. But I should never make you feel like that's the only reason we're together. You know you're the prettiest girl in town. Who else could I date?" He said.

As far as apologies go, it wasn't the best. But at least he was being honest.

"That's okay," I said. "I forgive you."

Michael beamed. "Groovy." He thrust the package in my arms. "I also got this for you as an 'I'm sorry' present."

Under the crisp gold paper was a brown cardboard shoebox, the lid carefully sealed.

"Open it up," Michael said. He could barely contain his excitement.

Inside was a gorgeous baseball glove made of the softest, butteriest kip leather the color of roasted almonds. The lacing matched the Lady Scarlet uniforms and my number was embroidered on the palm in crimson stitching.

My heart sang. This was it! Michael was telling me it was okay to still play baseball, that he would love me even if I went out West to pursue my dream instead of following my parents' plan. I could scream or cry with happiness. I threw my arms around him, jumping up and down with joy.

"Thank you!" I said, choking back sobs. "I love it, I do!"

"Do you?" He asked, strangely. Normally Michael was so confident. "I wasn't sure about the size."

"Oh, it should be fine, my hands are small enough to fit any glove," I said.

To emphasize my point, I slipped it on. But it got stuck. I stared down, puzzled. The glove was at least three inches shorter than it should be. It was child-sized! Inwardly, I groaned in disappointment. There was no way I could ever use this beautiful glove. What a waste. Dammit, Michael. Why hadn't he gotten some help with sizing? Who in the world convinced him anyone could use a glove this small? It was made for little league, not college ball.

My face gave me away.

"Something wrong?" Michael asked.

"It's just... it's a little smaller than the one I normally use. I can make it work though," I said, to save the moment.

Michael laughed.

"But it's not for you, Bliss!"

I shook my head in confusion.

"But who is it for? These are my colors. This is my number!"

Michael hugged me. "I thought one day our son could use it. You know, to honor his mother's high school career as state champion."

I went numb. To fight back the ocean of tears that threatened to spill out and drown us all, I concentrated on tracing the number on the palm of the glove and counting back from 10. There was no way I would humiliate myself by crying in public. I forced myself to show my teeth in a gruesome approximation of a smile. I got a present. You smile when someone gives you a present.

"See, Bliss? Softball isn't over. It's going to live on in the next generation. I'm so happy you like it," he said.

Michael didn't have a single goddamn clue. Stupid Michael. But why should he know what I wanted? It's not like I was ever truly honest with him. Instead, I kept my hopes and dreams secret, shoving them far out of sight where they couldn't interfere with my family's expectations. I just kept fake smiling instead of speaking my mind.

Stupid Michael. It was easier to blame him than face a harder truth: Stupid, stupid Bliss.

Chapter 36

Michael left and I walked back to the salon in a daze.

"Manicure time!" Cher chirped and I took my seat next to Peggy.

I was hollowed out, a shell of a girl. I shouldn't have believed for a second that Michael would support me going to Arizona. I was an idiot. Better to be totally resigned to my life than to count on even an ounce of hope. Because having it ripped away felt like the worst home plate collision of my life. It was worse than striking out during that horrible game. Hope was the mistake of letting my heart feel something again only to have it crushed. I was through making that mistake.

Listlessly, I offered up one hand then another to be buffed and filed, polished and dried.

Peggy kept up a steady stream of conversation before eventually giving up.

"Bliss!" she said while I sat silently, waiting for my nails to dry. We'd picked matching shades of blush.

"What?" I asked. "I mean, pardon?" I said, remembering my debutante manners.

We were alone together in the salon. Cher and the other girl had moved onto other customers while our nail polish set.

"I know this isn't what you want," Peggy said.

If anyone could see right through me, it was my best friend. There was no point lying or trying to convince her she was wrong. But what was I going to say? I smiled sadly.

"Wouldn't it be easier if it were?" I asked.

Chapter 37

I was the teenage dream.

I shone like a new penny in my ivory taffeta gown. My copper hair gleamed under the twinkling lights, my emerald eyes sparkled. I smiled at my flawless friends, waved to my darling parents, took the arm of my escort — the most dashing partner at this year's Cotillion Ball, everyone said. I was the picture of beauty and grace.

My life was perfect.

Maybe if I said it enough times, I'd start to believe the lie.

The decorating committee had outdone itself this year. Not a single one of Mama's hated carnation anywhere. The club was bursting with calla lilies and candles, the regular dining room transformed from after-tennis snack bar to a gala venue. All the members were in their good tuxes, their wives in designer gowns.

Backstage, Michael handed me my bouquet and smiled. I mustered up a weak grin in return. I would have preferred the carnations. The bright, hardy flowers made me think of summer days at the ballpark. Not like Mama's lilies, with pristine white petals that betrayed nothing. They were kind of like the perfect debutante that way.

"Are you ready to make your debut, Miss Bliss Bennet?" Michael asked.

"Sure," I said, with minimum enthusiasm. Just one more to-do item on my life's checklist.

"Don't worry, baby, you'll knock them dead."

I squeezed his hand. It was nice of him to mistake my apathy for nerves. I don't bother telling him that I don't have anything left to be nervous about. It was smooth sailing from here on out, my course expertly charted by Mama and Daddy.

Michael kissed me gently and I reminded myself again how lucky I was that he was my boyfriend. He was a man made to wear a tuxedo, the sharp lines of the suit molding to his lean frame and highlighting his chiseled features. His mop of dark hair had been slicked back and rested perfectly in place.

Every girl here with a borrowed date would have killed for Michael as an escort, but my focus was on someone else. I scanned the club for the Jem. It shouldn't be hard to find the only non-white person here.

Around me, my fellow debutantes made last-minute adjustments, patting down hair and boosting up cleavage. I didn't bother to fix anything. Mama made sure I was flawless.

Not that I particularly cared about any of that right now. I strained my eyes peering into dark corners, searching for the face I wanted to see. This was my last chance to tell Jem I was sorry. I owed him that much, at least.

Waiters bustled in and out on the way to the kitchen, and I peered at each one, hoping for Jem. I was grateful Michael had mistaken my wild-eyed distraction for butterflies. Like there was anything hard about walking out on stage after someone called your name. I'd already had the most epic strike out of my life in front of the whole country. There was nothing in the world left for me to be embarrassed about.

Michael slings his arm around me and kisses my neck. I close my eyes and try to pretend that I like the way it felt. When I open my eyes again, I spot him.

Jem stands across the room, clutching a tray of drinks and staring at me. My stomach knots and twists. How much had he seen? I didn't want him to think... I didn't want him to think what? That I was with my boyfriend? That I wasn't going out West with him? All my truths were disappointments. I needed to explain myself. He needed to know that my decision had nothing to do with him.

I push Michael's arm off my shoulders and moved towards Jem, but he's gone in an instant. I could probably catch up to him if I ran.

"Bliss, where are you going?" Michael asked, confused. "They're calling us now."

Michael offered me his hand and after a moment's hesitation, I took it. I followed him to wait for our cue. I had my chance to talk to Jem but I blew it. Once more, I chose to do what was expected from me instead of what my heart was calling me to do. I wasn't sure I could take a lifetime of this.

Chapter 38

Thanks to The Popps my introduction and short waltz were flawless. I beamed for the photographer without once letting the smile go to my eyes. My footwork was perfection. Not a single stumble, not even when I waved back at Mama's grinning face or craned my neck in every which direction to spot Jem again.

"You're just absolutely golden, the two of you sweethearts together," Mama said. "That was just perfection."

I squeezed her hand.

"Thanks, Mama."

I hated being a deb, but I didn't hate seeing Mama happy. All of this nonsense was worth it to see her out of the house with lipstick on. She was why I couldn't leave. It would break her heart.

"And isn't just the most wonderful night. I swear the stars just go on forever," Mama said.

Mama and her stars. The stars! That was it. I knew exactly where Jem was. Where he liked to go when he needed space to think.

"Now where did your Daddy get to?" Mama asked. "We need to find that photographer and have a family portrait taken. It's important that we remember this night."

I couldn't hang around now that I had figured out where Jem was. I scrambled for an excuse to get away.

"Yes, Mama. But I, uh, just need to powder my nose first. I don't want to be shiny in the photo!"

Mama nodded approvingly, thinking I was finally taking all her beauty advice to heart. I scurried in the direction of the bathroom and paused at the door, checking on Mama. She'd found the photographer and was straightening Daddy's bowtie. While she was distracted, I continued down the hall to the fire escape.

My heels clattered on the cement steps. Impatient, I hoisted my dress to run faster. I couldn't risk missing Jem again. I should have known he would be out on the roof. It's where all of our important moments happened.

Heart pounding, I burst through the door and onto the moonlit roof, expecting Jem in his rumpled cater waiter outfit. Instead there was only debris. Cigarette butts and the petals from some discarded bouquet.

Winded, I gripped the rusted door handle to steady myself. I so badly wanted Jem to be there. But I should have known by now that hope only leaves you hollowed out when you realized you could never have what you want.

My shoulders sagged in defeat. I stopped in the staircase to compose my face and reset my posture, rolling my shoulders back into place. I pinched my cheeks to bring the flush back to

the skin. Happy, happy, smiling, shiny, happy, perfect, I reminded myself. Happy, happy, happy
You loved your life. You loved your life. You loved your life. Why did I feel like I wanted to die

I took a deep breath and stepped back into the ball.

"There she is," a voice said, relieved. "Kid, we've been looking all over for ya."

I whirled at the familiar sound.

"Coach? What are you doing here?"

It definitely wasn't for the Cotillion Ball. Coach wore his usual outfit of tracksuit and
sneakers. Next to him, grim-faced, was Eli Richmond, the deputy sheriff, awkward in his stiff
brown uniform. What on earth was going on? This was going to give the club something to talk
about.

"We need you to come with us right away, Bennet. Something urgent has come up and it
involves you."

Chapter 39

F rom nowhere, Mama appeared at my elbow.

"Go somewhere? I don't think so, Wilfred," she said to Coach. "It's time for the father-daughter dance. Go on, Bliss, before your father gets cross."

When I didn't move, Mama gave me a gentle shove in the direction of the dance floor where Daddy waited for me. He cleaned up nicely tonight, the gold cuff links Mama had bought him for his birthday gleaming at his wrists. After a summer of practice, I could do the short waltz steps in my sleep. Good thing, since my mind swirled with the summons from Coach and the deputy sheriff. I'd never been in trouble with the law before. What could I have possibly done? Was this because I'd kissed Jem? No, I only felt like I should go to jail for that. It wasn't actually illegal. My palms prickled with sweat.

"You look beautiful tonight," Daddy said.

I barely heard him, my mind churning with paranoid thoughts. Was this about the tournament? Maybe they thought I struck out on purpose?

Daddy repeated himself and I murmured my thanks. We danced in silence. I didn't have a whole lot to say to Daddy these days. Our stiff steps were a far cry from when he used to bring me to family dances at the club and I'd stand on his feet while he spun us around the room.

Daddy cleared his throat.

"You know, your mother and I are so proud of you. We are so pleased to see you off to Bryn Mawr in the fall. We just know you'll make the best co-ed," he said.

"I'm glad that you're happy, Daddy," I said automatically.

That's why I was doing this. To make them proud. I finally met his eyes. To my surprise, they shimmered with tears.

"You know, Bliss, we always let your mother take the credit for your unusual name because it wouldn't do for a man to appear soft like that, but I was the one who chose it," he said.

What? That was news to me.

There were complications with my birth, he told me. The doctors thought that Mama and I might die during the delivery.

I was stunned. This was the first I'd ever heard of this. As far as I knew, everything about my birth was just as pleasant and normal as the rest of my life to date.

"Why did no one tell me this before?" I asked.

"You didn't need to know how hard it was for you to get here. You were just here. When the nurses finally swaddled you and handed the little bundle to me, I saw my complete family together in the room and I declared that I had 'found my bliss.' The nurses asked if that's what we were naming you, and Marie said yes," he said.

Daddy rested his cheek on top of my head. "From that moment, I swore I would protect and guide you no matter what. I wanted that day in the hospital to be the worst day of your life, and you never even had to know about it. Now you're heading off to a good school, you're going steady with a nice man, and I couldn't be prouder of you or of the job that we've done raising you," he said.

My eyes stung. This was the Daddy I remembered from better days. He was so really, truly happy that I knew I'd made the right decision. Staying here in my place was what was right. If only I had the chance to explain that to Jem. This was why I couldn't go with him. I needed to tell him that before he left.

I hugged Daddy tight as the song ended. It was nice to be held like a little girl again. It reminded me of when things were easier. When I just did what I was told, and Mama and Daddy could give me everything I wanted. I wished I could just stay in that moment forever, to be simply happy and free from wanting things I couldn't have.

Eli coughed awkwardly, ruining my peaceful reverie. He stood before us, trying to emit authority, Mama nervously hovering behind him. All tenderness dropped from Daddy's face.

"Bliss needs to come with us," he said timidly.

Daddy glared.

"Uh, please, sir," Eli added. That chicken. Eli's Daddy was the real sheriff and everyone, including Eli, knew that he would never quite measure up.

"What exactly do you think is so urgent that you need to take my daughter away in the middle of her debutante ball?" Daddy asked, his eyes tiny pinpricks to disdain.

Eli shifts uncomfortably. Any authority he may have channelled for the night has long fled under the beam of Daddy's hot scrutiny.

"It's a matter of national security, sir," Eli said.

"I am waiting for you to enlighten me on what exactly this has to do with my teenage daughter," Daddy said.

Eli took two steps forward and lowered his voice. "We may have a lead on the softball spy," he said.

The sign stealer! The person who'd cost us the tournament and crushed my dreams. All of a sudden, I felt like I couldn't get enough air into my lungs. My breathing was shallow and fast. I needed to know who it was.

Chapter 40

Peeople were starting to stare at the disruption on the dance floor. The ruffled collar of Mama's gown quivered with her nerves. She clutched Daddy's elbow with whitened fingers.

"Chip, I think we're starting to make a scene," she murmured. "Why don't we just go outside and hear what they have to say?"

"Oh, for God's sake, Marie," he snapped, shaking her off. "This is ridiculous."

Instantly, Coach was at Mama's side. "I can assure you, it is not," Coach said in a hard voice I'd never heard him use before. He and Daddy glared hot daggers at each other for an uncomfortable minute. Mama's eyes rolled nervously.

"We aren't going anywhere," Daddy said.

I panicked. If we didn't go, we weren't going to find out who had stolen the signals. I couldn't let that happen.

"Oh yes, we are," I said, turning heel and striding for the exit. I didn't wait to see if they were following me or not.

The night was hot as I stepped outside. Katydid chirps filled the air. The valet attendant turned to me, taking in my red hair.

"Bliss?" He asked, unsure.

"That's me," I said.

"Oh, that's a relief. Jem left this for you," he said, extending a folded note. "His shift is over and he asked me to give this to you."

Before I could read it over, Daddy busted through the doors with Mama hanging off his arm, Eli and Coach hot on his heels. I tucked the note into the top of my dress.

"Take a hike, son" Coach told the valet attendant in his good-natured way.

"You've gotten me outside," Daddy said. "Spit it out."

"We've had a defector," Eli whispered.

"A what?" I said. I couldn't hear him.

"A defector!" Daddy boomed. "You know, like that poor fool who jumped off the ship to get into America."

Kudirka. He was on the news. He leapt right off his Soviet ship onto a U.S. Coast Guard vessel. I was shocked and proud at the same time. Our country was so amazing, people would risk life and limb to get in.

Now a teenage Soviet softball player had done the same.

"But they all seemed so loyal," I said.

Fiercely loyal to the Soviet way of life. Mocking our American greed and selfishness. Which girl decided to abandon those ideals? It was hard to imagine.

"Not all of them, it turns out," Eli said.

"Chalk another one up for the U.S.A.," Daddy said, his voice taking on that warning tone I knew so well. "But I still don't know what this has to do with us and frankly, I'm getting tired of your games."

Coach stepped in.

"Chip, one of our girls was passing along information to the Soviets during the tournament. This girl says she can finger the traitor."

"So who is it?" I asked, impatient for answers.

"Well, the thing is, there's a catch," said Coach.

"Tell me!" I said, nearly bursting from my skin.

"She says she'll only talk to Bliss."

Chapter 41

"Forget it," Daddy said.

Did he really think he could keep me away from finding out the truth? My heart pounded in my chest. I whirled on him.

"I'm going, Daddy," I said. "I need to know who blew the tournament for us. You can't protect me from everything."

For a full minute, Daddy was silent while my hands trembled in defiance. I stood my ground. I was doing everything else that they asked of me, but I needed to find out this truth for myself, no matter what Daddy said. Finally, he blinked.

"Fine, but I'm going with you," he said.

I smiled. It felt good to get my way.

Eli, Coach, Daddy and I piled into Eli's cruiser. Mama tried to get in too, but Daddy blocked her. But she wasn't listening to him either.

"Oh no, y'all aren't running off to do God knows what without me," she said.

Daddy pleaded with her to stay.

"Please, Marie. All this excitement will only upset you," he said.

Mama's eyes flashed dangerously. She drew herself up to every last inch of her height, her perfect posture rigid. I can't remember the last time I'd seen her look like that.

"I'm coming," she said. "And you fools can't stop me."

Daddy was silent. Mama had been so fragile for so long that it was easy to forget how strong she could be. I was proud of her. This was the Mama that I knew. The pushy one who got lilies instead of carnations. The one who went wherever she damned well pleased.

Coach sat in the front while Daddy, Mama, and I squeezed into the back. Sandwiched between them, I'm eight years old again. Eli nattered to fill the otherwise oppressive silence of the ride.

"We picked her up this afternoon after she got caught stealing from the Minimart," Eli said. "Seemed like she did a runner before her team was meant to leave. Been living rough for the past week. Made her way here."

Eli pulled into the Sheriff's spot right outside the station's doors.

"How long is your Father gone for?" Mama asked.

The tips of Eli's ears colored. Mama could spot when someone was playing at being something they weren't. It was a miracle she hadn't seen through me yet.

Eli cleared his throat nervously. He ignored Mama's question and kept talking.

"She's in a holding cell now," Eli said. "When Bliss is ready, she can go in to see her."

"Is it safe?" Mama asked.

"Oh yes, the girl doesn't seem inclined to violence. After all, she wants to stay here and live free. But we'll be watching just outside the door, just in case," Eli replied.

I moved up the stairs and down the quiet hallway, struggling to control my breathing. My toes curled in anticipation of what I was about to learn. Why me? Why was I the only one the girl would speak with? It was only when Mama held my hand to warm my cold fingers that I realized just how hard they were shaking. Her comfort soothed me.

An officer stood guard outside the holding room.

"You ready, Bliss?" Eli asked.

I wouldn't let my anxiety show. I'd had my dreams crushed and managed to live through it. There was no reason to be afraid now. I straightened my dress, patted down my hair, and adjusted my long white gloves. Whatever this girl wanted from me, we weren't the same. The tournament was over and nothing could touch me anymore.

The guard stepped aside and Eli keyed in the code for the door. I squared my shoulders and stepped in.

The girl's back was turned, but I would recognize that tiny powerful body anywhere. That dark hair. She faced me. There were shadows under her eyes, but they glinted as bright as ever. Her jail-issued jumpsuit did nothing to drop that proud chin.

"Valentina," I said.

I wasn't surprised. Not really.

She smiled, showing her pointy teeth.

"Bliss," she said. "You came."

Chapter 42

V alentina roved her eyes over my long white gloves, the pearly shine of my ball gown. Even the harsh florescent lighting couldn't diminish my glow of beauty and privilege.

It was a stark contrast from Valentina. She wore a grease-stained shapeless beige jumpsuit that made her skin look sallow. Her hair was unwashed and pulled back into a harsh bun. She'd bitten her nails to the quick, her fingers raw from worry. She was reduced, but unbowed. Despite her surroundings, her eyes burned as brightly as ever. Her spine was as straight as any dream debutante's.

I braced myself for a tirade, but instead, she delivered her words with kindness.

"Ah," she said. "I was right. You truly are an American princess, no? I can always spot rich girls."

She swept her hand forward casually, inviting me to take the extra folding chair across from her as if she were the hostess at a society party. I sat primly, removing my gloves and fiddling with my ring. Valentina's sharp eyes missed nothing. They lit on the sparkling jewel.

"This is new, is it not? A gift from your man. But which one? Did you pick between them? Such a difficult decision: The wealthy one in the sharp suit or the one who loves you as much as he loves baseball?"

My stomach tightened and I was immediately defensive.

"What do you know about it?" I asked.

She shrugged indifferently. "I know what I see. The one who takes you out for fancy dinners is from your world. He is the one you are meant to be with, no?"

How well she understood me just by observation. Her words weren't cruel, just matter of fact. In spite of myself, I answered.

"Yes, that's my boyfriend, Michael. He gave me this. It's a promise ring," I said.

"So he has staked his claim. But what about Jem? The strong one. Have you broken his heart?"

Valentina's face was a little too eager for my answer. I remembered how she flirted with him in the dining hall. She wanted him for herself and it pissed me off. Even if I'd chosen Michael. Not that I could blame her. If my life were different, would Jem be the one I was meant to be with?

"It's not like that with us. We're friends, that's all," I said.

Except that I'm not sure I can even call Jem a friend anymore. My posture falters with sadness.

Valentina puffed out a laugh.

"I have seen the way he looks at you. Like you are some kind of divine creature he has the good fortune of spotting on earth," she said.

"I doubt that," I said.

I tensed at the memory of my last conversation with Jem. Our fight before the game. The anger on his face. The stinging slap of my palm on his cheek. The hurt in his eyes as I stormed away. No, I couldn't even call him my friend anymore.

"Maybe you are blind to what is in front of you," Valentina said. "But I cannot blame you for making the smart choice. Michael is a provider. You will never be hungry with him."

What a strange thing to say. I'd never been hungry in my life. Valentina's sharp cheekbones hinted that hunger might be something she knew a thing or two about. Was that why she was here? Because America was a better provider than the Soviet Union?

I bristled at her words. What was she saying about me? That my motives were mercenary? That my decisions were driven by my finances? My choices were about more than money. They were driven by expectations. I'd picked the right man based on the rules of my world.

What the hell business of Valentina's was it anyway? Just a month ago she was my sworn enemy, now she sat across from me in a goddamn holding cell trying to make pronouncements about my life. She should try out a mirror sometime. She was a traitor to her country, a defector. Not much honor there. At least I had loyalty. I was with Michael first and I stayed with Michael, no matter what other temptation I might have faced.

I huffed impatiently. Valentina had an unparalleled talent for getting under my skin. This talk was supposed to be about the traitor on Team USA, the betrayer who gave our signs up to the Soviets. Not about my love life or Jem's feelings for me.

"What do you want anyway?" I asked. "Why am I even here? I thought you hated me."

Valentina smiled serenely.

"I never hated you," she said. "I was hardest on you because you were my biggest competition. The star hitter versus the star pitcher. I wanted to rattle you. It worked, did it not?"

Sure, but what did it even matter anymore? That was all behind me now. If I was going to move on with my life, I needed to make peace with softball.

"So what? What am I even here for anyway?" I pulled my gloves on, getting ready to leave.

Valentina didn't have any power over me. I could walk away from this conversation at any time. Her supposed inside information was obviously just a ploy to lure me here for one last jab.

"I wanted to tell you it wasn't your fault."

I froze. The guilt and frustration, the pain and disappointment I had tried to forget came crashing back to me. My heart contracted and tears sprung to my eyes. I blinked back hot wetness. My knees weakened and I tumbled back into the chair. I waited for Valentina to continue.

Chapter 43

"**I**t wasn't your fault," Valentina repeated.

I wasn't sure I was ready for what she had to say. I'd spent the past week pushing those memories deep down inside me. Shoving them into those boxes in my mind attic, willing them away, convinced I had made the right choice. I couldn't dredge all those painful thoughts back now. I didn't trust myself not to ruin my makeup, for one thing.

I said nothing and played with the palms of my hands. The callouses I'd built up there over a season of batting practice were fading under Mama's ministrations. A lady's hands should always be smooth, she said. I argued that I would be wearing gloves at the Cotillion Ball anyway, but she seemed determined to wipe all last remaining evidence of my softball days away.

Valentina didn't push her point. I wasn't ready to hear her yet. I should have just left, but I was rooted in the hard metal chair. Drawn to her presence, craving some kind of explanation for what happened.

"Why'd you defect anyway?" I asked, tracing the lines on my creamy palms with my melon-pink nails.

If I could have chosen anyone on the Soviet team to defect it wouldn't have been Valentina, the militant pitcher and team leader. She was the most disciplined, the most focused, the one who wanted the win the worst. I couldn't believe that she just walked away from it all.

"Maybe I want to be American Princess, too," she said.

Her wry smile teased me. I was the one in the designer gown while she wore a prison jumpsuit. But Valentina controlled our meeting. She would not be bowed for long.

I rolled my eyes at her.

"Ha, ha," I said. "Very funny. But I'm pretty sure you would love for me to know, so why don't you just tell me?"

Something strange hit me: I may just be Valentina's only friend in the whole world. And calling us friends was a stretch.

"Do you like softball?" Valentina asked.

The simple question was a dagger to my heart.

"I love it," I finally whispered. "I'm trying not to anymore."

"I hate it," Valentina said.

I shake my head. How could the most ferocious player on the field not like playing?

"Why would you play a game you hate?" I asked.

Why would anyone dedicate so much time to a game she couldn't stand?

Valentina laughed. The sound was hollow.

"Do you know what it feels like to be hungry?" She asked.

"Sure," I said, remembering long drives home after a game or a hard workout, spent with an empty stomach. Aching to get home so I could devour whatever Rosa had prepared.

"No, you have known only American hunger. The twinge that your belly feels when it is not constantly full," Valentina said. "I know what the real starvation feels like."

"I thought the Mother Country made sure everyone was well-fed," I said, sarcastically.

Valentina's laugh turned into a bitter bark.

"When something works so hard to appear perfect it is because there are many things wrong. It is easier to present as flawless than to do the work of repairing those flaws. This is how it is in the Soviet Union," Valentina said.

I pursed my lips. She may as well be talking about Mama and Daddy. Or me. But all the hairspray and lipstick in the world couldn't cover up what was wrong with me inside. Or make up for my loss.

Valentina's eyes took on a dreamy quality. She was lost in memory.

"I am from a village so small you will not find it on a map. I live there with my Mother and Father. We are farmers until there is an accident and Father loses his hand. His new best friend is vodka. Mother tries to work, but Father is too drunk to show her how. I am only little girl. Nine. Too small too work. We cannot make our quota and they reduce our rations. The authorities take everything and leave us with a few rotten bags of grain. It is winter. Mother tries to make it last, but it is not enough. The neighbors help some, but they do not have much.

I make a new friend too. She follows me to school every day. Pokes me when I try to learn my lessons. Trips me when I try to play outside. Crawls into bed with me at night and holds me so close I cannot sleep. I will do anything to make her go away. Suck on rocks, peel bark off trees, steal lunches from other children, but still, she stays. She climbs on my back, gets into my soul. She gets heavier and heavier and every day it becomes harder to carry her. One day, I cannot anymore and I collapse on the way home from school."

Valentina was starving to death. Goosebumps raised on my forearms. Her description chilled me, the casual way she told a story about dying.

"What happened?" I asked.

"My teacher finds me on her way home. Asleep in the snow, blue all over. She picks me up and carries me to her house. She puts me in the bath, warms me up. And then she gives me a bowl of stew so big I could not finish. My dark friend disappeared."

Valentina smiled at the memory.

"She has no husband and no children. I am her new pet. She brings me food to eat. Takes me home when it is cold. And she teaches me how to play this new game she saw in a movie once. Baseball. The Americans love it, her brother tells her. He is from our village too, but he lives in Moscow now. He is in government and getting powerful. He wants more children to play baseball, to show Americans the strength of Soviet Russia, at whatever game they choose.

One day, the brother watches me play. My teacher wants to show him how I can throw straight and hard. He leaves to make a phone call and comes back with a suitcase for me. He says that I am now moving to Leningrad, to go to sports school. He takes me to say goodbye to Mother and Father. He says that I will return at break. I never return."

Sports school. That must be those training centres you hear about, the awful ones where small children are either molded into perfect future Olympic athletes or sent home in disgrace. My stomach twisted at tiny Valentina being shipped off far from home and never coming back. The horrible pressure she must have been under, whether she realized it or not.

"Didn't your parents say something? How can they just take you away like that?" I asked, horrified.

I imagined being sent far from Mama and Daddy, likely to never see them again. I panicked, forgetting that I so very nearly made that choice for myself by going to Arizona. Valentina shrugged. It was a deep motion of acceptance for the way things were done.

"Russia is not like America. You do not say *nyet* to the government. Only *da*. Yes. Always, yes. It is a great honor to be chosen for sports school and my parents were compensated. They are not hungry anymore. And neither am I. Every day I go to bed with a full belly. For the first time in my life. I have never seen so much bread. My first week there, I cry every night because I am so happy, you see? I am safe and warm and my little friend is banished. As long as I play baseball, I am fine. I am good and I am lucky," she said.

I loved softball. The smell of the hot dirt and cut grass. The taste of concession stand bubble gum. The way each time at bat was a new chance to do something great. But I didn't need to play. The game wasn't my lifeboat. Not the way it was for Valentina. No wonder she had fire in her eyes when she played. It was her meal ticket. Her future depended on it. Kind of like Linda. She played with a ferocity that came from knowing all of their tomorrows were wrapped up in today's game.

Was it possible to resent something you depended on for survival? Is that why Valentina hated softball? Or said she did? But Linda didn't hate softball. No matter what she'd said. She came alive when she played.

"So why do you hate softball? Why did you leave?" I asked.

Valentina met my gaze and held it for a long time.

"I only know one thing: Winning games. Throwing ball fast, hitting it hard. I have no friends. No boyfriend. No life. From the moment I arrive in Leningrad, I am a child no more. Only a tool to prove Soviet might. There is no school at sports school. Only English lessons. I have no knowledge. Only baseball. And now I am trapped. What will I do when they are done with me? Go back to my village? Learn how to farm? Or will I join the Party? Find other little girls and take away their childhoods? I cannot do that."

Valentina's steely resolve started to crumble. Her voice broke and wavered. She fought back tears.

"But my friend waits for me. She is patient. In the shadows, hoping for weakness. Only doing exactly what I am told keeps her away. So you see, in USSR, my whole life is already laid out for me. And I have no choice because I am... so... so afraid of my friend."

Valentina's tears flowed in earnest now. I fought the impulse to hug her tight. She wouldn't like me acknowledging her weakness. Instead, I sat patiently while she recovered.

Valentina wiped her face roughly with the back of her hands. She smeared the tears on her jumpsuit and composed herself. Her bright eyes glittered with resolve. Her pointy chin raised once more. It was an unspoken agreement between us: the crying never happened.

"Why did I defect?" She asked. "I left because I do not want to be afraid anymore. I want freedom. The freedom to be who I am instead of who the sports bureau demands. In America, I will be myself."

Her voice was so hopeful and determined that I couldn't bring myself to correct her. She would find out eventually, on her own.

You didn't always get to be yourself, even in the Land of the Free.

Chapter 44

Someone rapped on the door. Valentina and I stared at each other.

"Just a moment," she said, imperiously.

Who the hell was she to be giving orders? But there she was, acting like she was still in charge. That was Valentina through and through.

Valentina shifted forward in her seat and took my hand. I tried not to flinch under her touch. I saw myself through her eyes. A spoiled, selfish girl. A silly girl, too afraid to stand up for what she wanted. Not like Valentina, who was brave enough to risk the wrath of two counties. She left everything she had ever known behind and chased her dream. Next to her, I was pathetic. She was everything I was not.

"It is not your fault, Bliss," she said again. "I see in your eyes, you are defeated. Not just in baseball, but in your spirit."

"Oh, what do you know about it?" I said, tearing my hand away.

I couldn't stand to have her read me like this. She was one of the only people in the world who had a clue about who I really was.

A single tear slid down my cheek.

"It was my fault," I said.

If only I hadn't been so foolish. If I'd played it safe instead of swinging for the fences. I tried to be the hero and I let everyone down. Especially myself.

"No, it is not," Valentina said gently. "Baseball is team sport. Russians understand this. Every out is of equal importance. The third out just ends it all. If you strike out first, you would not be blaming yourself this way for your loss."

I paused. I'd never seen it that way, but it was true. I wouldn't be beating myself up if I had struck out first.

"You are a fierce competitor, I know this," Valentina said. "It takes time, but one day you will forgive yourself. You must."

I wasn't entirely convinced, but there was no time to argue. Someone knocked again, more insistently this time.

"Yes?" I said.

Eli popped his head in, biting his lip.

"Say, Bliss. Have you gotten the name of the spy yet?"

Oh right, that was why I was here. Not to sort through my personal issues.

"Not yet," I said.

Eli shifted from foot to foot.

"Well, hurry up, would you? The CIA is on its way to talk to her and, uh, well, getting a teenage girl to do an interrogation is not exactly standard procedure, if you know what I mean," he said.

"Sure, Eli," I said. "I'll hurry up."

Eli left. Valentina sat peacefully, unruffled by the news that the CIA was about to come and take her away. Who knew what would happen to her.

"Well," I said, my heart racing. "This is why I'm here. Tell me who it was."

Valentina smirked.

"It is your own Nancy Bell."

Chapter 45

I laughed, the crazed laughed of a nutjob. I couldn't help it. I'd come unhinged. This was one last sick joke from Valentina. She couldn't possibly be telling the truth. Nancy Bell? Nancy "My uncle is a commie hunter and we'll destroy you for being UnAmerican" Bell? No. No way. No how.

"You're kidding," I said, suddenly angry. My face flushed with rage.

"I assure you, I am not," Valentina replied.

"Why the hell would Nancy Bell give away our signals to the Soviets?" I said.

Valentina held her hands out like a set of scales.

"We need information, and she needs money. It is a perfect match," she said, making her hands go up and down to weigh both sides.

I couldn't get my mind around it. Nancy Bell was one of the richest girls in town. Why would she ever need to do anything for money?

"You must be confusing Nancy with someone else," I said. "Dark hair, drives the t-bird, stuck up. She plays left field? Is that who you mean?"

Valentina smiled like a well-fed cat.

"I am not mistaken. Nancy gives us the information we need."

"But why? I can't believe it," I said. I couldn't process her words.

"Why is it that you Americans can never believe when someone betrays you?" She asked. "The answer is simple: greed. We do our research on all the players and their families. The Bells have money problems."

"More than Linda's?" I asked. I hated myself for sounding just like Daddy.

Valentina arched her brow at me. See? She said with her eyes, you really were a spoiled princess.

"Linda has a nice family," Valentina said. "They make enough money and they live within their means. It is a simple life, but an honest one. Not like what do you call them? Debuts?"

"Debutantes," I corrected automatically.

Valentina waved my word away dismissively, her disgust clear.

"Nancy's family wants a certain lifestyle. House, car, dresses, jewels, balls. But they cannot afford that lifestyle. Lots of debts. Lots of bad people calling. We make them go away. Easy." Valentina snapped her fingers.

I flushed. Goddamn Nancy Bell! I would be packed for Arizona right now if it weren't for her! Why did she have to shove her wealth in everyone's face? We'd probably like her better if she weren't always talking about how much money she had.

"Right, all she had to do was betray her country and sell out her team," I said. Sarcasm dripped from my voice.

Valentina shrugged again. Her cool was infuriating.

"American Princess, you know nothing about wanting. About how desperate makes you. Nancy does what she needs to survive," she said.

"That's bullshit," I said.

"It is the truth," Valentina said, locking eyes with mine. They burned fiercely with her next words. "Will you do what you need to survive?"

Eli knocked desperately. Our time was up. I needed to leave. Valentina raised her chin again, arms crossed in her threadbare jumpsuit. What could I say to this girl? My nemesis turned defector. The girl who could see right through me.

"Good luck," I said.

I walked out of the interrogation room and didn't look back. Daddy and Eli waited for me. Eli was worried. The skin around her nails was raw from where he'd been chewing them. Daddy nervously puffed a cigarette. He stubbed it out angrily when I emerged.

"Well?" Eli asked. "What did she say?"

Where did I even start?

Eli pressed me. "We need a name, Bliss."

Poor, stupid, Nancy Bell. Turned traitor because her family tried so hard to be something they weren't. Whose fault was it really? Theirs? Or ours for maintaining a ridiculous standard of what it meant to be the right kind of people?

"This is serious now," Daddy said. "Tell the man what he needs to know."

I considered his words. Daddy re-lit another cigarette. They wanted me to name names, finger the culprit. That would be the proper thing to do. That was what they expected of me, the perfect daughter. To give them what they wanted, cast blame and walk away. But what would telling the truth about Nancy really do? Ruin her life, probably. For something that was already done. If she thought she had to betray her country just to help her parents out of debt, Nancy's life was already a shambles. Those work-study applications weren't a joke. She really was going to end up as a cafeteria server. Sadly, the thought didn't give me the same amount of satisfaction it would have a month ago. Nancy didn't need any more shit. It wouldn't come from me. I was tired of playing their game.

"No," I said.

"No?" Asked Daddy. His eyes bulged with anger.

"No," I said again and turned away from him.

"Bliss Bennet, don't you dare walk away from me," he said.

My heart thumped loudly in my chest, I'd never openly defied Daddy like this before.

"Or what?" I asked, my nostrils flared, challenging him. "What are you going to do to me? I already do everything you say."

Daddy couldn't take anything away from me because I didn't have anything I cared about anymore.

"We are going home, young lady," he said, clutching my arm. He snapped his fingers at Eli. "Get the car ready. You're driving us."

Daddy frog marched me around the station, hollering for Mama.

"Marie?" He yelled. "Where did you get to? We're leaving."

Daddy opened up a fire exit that led to a side alley. A flickering light illuminated a patch of crabgrass, trash-strewn and fenced in by chain link. Rats scurried along the side of the brick building.

A movement on the other side of a door caught my eye. Two figures moved together. I blinked my eyes once, twice, trying to shake out an image I couldn't believe. Coach and Mama, locked in a passionate embrace. My mind reeled. Suddenly, it all made sense. Why Mama let me play softball for so long. Why Daddy's face got so sour whenever someone mentioned Coach's name. How long has this been going on for? Was Coach the reason Mama was so sad? Or did he make her happy?

Daddy's grip on my arm tightened. "Marie?" He said. His breathing was fast and uneven.

Coach and Mama broke apart immediately. Guilty. Caught. Mama smoothed down her dishevelled chignon. So much pretending. Everyone was hiding something about who they were.

"Chip," Mama started to say, but she was too late.

Like a wild dog, Daddy had lunged at Coach. He punched him in the face and there was the sickening sound of breaking bone. Blood gushed from Coach's nose.

Mama was screaming hysterically as Daddy grabbed for Coach again.

"Stop it!" I screamed, pulling my hair. "Stop it right now!"

They all froze and looked at me. Daddy, panting, his greased forelock falling into his red-rimmed eyes. Mama, tears streaked down her face, mascara running in every direction. Coach, jacket torn and shirt stained with blood.

It was all a lie. The perfect home and family was just for show. Underneath was wanting, pain, and anger. It would happen to me too if I let Mama and Daddy turn me into them. I couldn't be their diamond girl anymore. Their perfect debutante daughter who followed every step laid out for her on a charmed path. Because I knew if I stayed, I would be contorting myself to fill the role in which they'd cast me. And if this horrible night had taught me anything, it was that masks could crack and the ugly truth would always be revealed in the end. I couldn't be who they wanted me to be.

This time, I turned to leave for good.

"Wait!" Mama said, grabbing my arm. "You don't understand, Bliss. What you saw there, was. Well, it was." She struggled to find the right words.

I held up my hands to stop her. "Mama. I don't care. I just want you to be happy."

I doubted she would ever let herself be. But I had to take a shot on myself.

I twisted the promise ring off my finger and passed it to Mama.

"Give this back to Michael, will you?" I asked.

Mama nodded mutely.

"I love you," I said, giving her one last kiss on the cheek and turned to leave.

It was time to follow my heart.

Chapter 46

My hand felt lighter without Michael's huge emerald weighing it down. I smiled at my bare finger. I couldn't wear jewelry on the field anyway. The air was sticky hot as I started the long walk home. After a few blocks, my feet cramped in my satin heels. I kicked them off with a grunt of satisfaction, leaving them orphaned on someone's front lawn.

Jem's note! In the excitement of the station, I'd completely forgotten. My throat tightened as I unfolded the paper.

The offer of a ride still stands. I'm leaving the school parking lot at midnight.

Midnight! What time was it now? Last I checked the clock at the station said 11 p.m. That was before the ruckus with Mama and Coach. I had no idea how much time had passed. I needed to move fast.

No more pretending. No more trying to be something I'm not. I was going to find Jem before he left and go with him.

I gathered up my dress in two hands, lifting the heavy folds above my knees and started to run.

I was sweaty and red-faced by the time I made it home. The front door was locked. Dammit! My key was in my clutch, which I'd left at the station. I stalked around the side of the house to the room window. Rosa liked to leave it open when she did washing to let the air in. With enough sweating and swearing, I managed to open it enough to fit my body. I eased my way through the window, slithering over the drier and landing in a heap on the floor.

I caught sight of myself in the mirror hanging off the back of the door. I was a deranged debutante. My chest heaved up and down trying to catch some air. My once glossy hair was tangled and undone, my creamy skin blotchy. I smiled. This was how I looked on the ball diamond.

I stripped off in the laundry room, leaving my dress and underthings. I sprinted naked upstairs to my room. Cotton underwear, sports bra, jeans, tee, sneakers, hat. I threw my clothes on like a woman possessed. My shirt might have been inside out but I didn't have time to check.

I grabbed a duffle bag and filled it with whatever was in reach. My room is a tornado of clothes and shoes. I double-checked that I had my glove. Everything else could be replaced. I had enough for a week, and surely Mama and Daddy would have cooled down enough by then to send me the rest of my clothes. Or maybe not, and I would actually have to learn how to use a washing machine.

I stopped at my door, trying to commit everything to memory. I stepped back to grab the silver-framed family photo, the one taken before Kathleen disappeared. They were still my family, even if I were rejecting them right now.

The grandfather clock in the living room chimed.

Dammit! It was midnight. My deadline. Jem said he'd be off by then.

Would he even be there when I arrived? I said I wasn't going, why would he wait around for a lost cause?

I still had to try. I owed that much to myself at least.

I snatched up my bag, tie my sneakers and start jogging to the school. I needed to make it. My legs pumped harder and faster until I was sprinting. My heart thudded in my chest and my lungs heaved for air, but I pushed through until I was at the edge of the baseball diamond.

My eyes strained in the darkness. Nothing. I collapsed in a heap, spent and defeated. Slowly, I hoisted myself up. At least I tried. I squinted again. There, in the bleachers, was movement. With a final burst of speed, I covered the last 100 yards.

Jem sat calmly as I strained for breath.

"I didn't think you were going to show," he said. His voice is casual, but a smile played at the corner of his lips. I gave him a goofy, sweaty grin.

It was just us and the katydids and the night. My future spread before me, infinite. My body hummed with possibility.

"You chose me," Jem said, softly. He put a calloused hand on my cheek. I flushed at his touch.

He took my bag and walked it to his Jeep. I followed behind, still catching my breath. This was just the beginning for us. I did choose him. But I also chose baseball. And freedom. And life.

"I chose myself," I whispered to the night.

Don't miss out!

Visit the website below and you can sign up to receive emails whenever Joni Harrison publishes a new book. There's no charge and no obligation.

https://books2read.com/r/B-A-GIUI-WSJBB

BOOKS 2 READ

Connecting independent readers to independent writers.

About the Author

Joni lives in Toronto with her husband and two children.
Read more at https://www.joniharrison.com.

Made in the USA
Middletown, DE
16 May 2023

30679658R00092